THE VISIONARY

Angeline Trevena

Bogus Caller Press

ISBN: 978-0-9934864-2-5

Cover art: Ben Farrow
Cover art copyright © 2016 Ben Farrow
www.estragonhelmer.com

Published by Bogus Caller Press
www.boguscallerpress.co.uk

Publisher's note:
The Visionary is a work of fiction. All names, characters, and places are the product of the author's imagination, used in fictitious manner. Any resemblances to actual persons, places, locales, events, etc. are purely coincidental.

THE HEAD

THE KEEP

THE EYE

NEWSTONE

THE WILLOWS

THE BAYS

THE BEECHES

THE BIRCHES

HEIGHT STREET

THE LAWNS

SALT STREET

HAVERHEAD

FORGE STREET

LYNSTOCK

THE CLUMP

THE GARDENS

HOPE STREET

BUCK WAY

WASH STREET

BRIDGE LANE

THE WATCH

SILK LANE

GUT ROAD

FOLD STREET

THE SWING

SATIN SQUARE

DUTIES

THE SALONS

SECOND STAIR

THE HOPE

NON LANE

TOP STREET

INLET ROAD

THE COMPOUND

NAVEL STREET

CRICK LANE

COMPOUND STREET

THE HIDE

THE DOWNS

HIND STREET

EYE STREET

HUNG STREET

OVERLOOK

TONGUE STREET

OVERLOOK

THE WALL

THE WALL

THE SQUEEZE

THE SLIP

THE FLOOR

POLL STREET

DOWNSTRIDE

THE CUBES

THE CUBES

THE EDGE

THE EDGE

FALWERE RIVER

1

There had been nothing exceptional about the evening. The flow of men had been steady, nothing out of the ordinary, and it had been a quiet night without incident. In fact, had Marianne kept a diary, she would have been hard pushed to think of anything to write in it.

But Marianne didn't keep a diary. She kept books of income and outgoings, she kept running totals, and stock levels, and she kept everyone sweet. She was one of those rare business owners who excelled with the finances, the employees, and the patrons.

Marianne was busy charming one of those patrons when everything started to fall apart. He was an old regular; almost from the day The Linden Tree had opened.

"Have another, Burl. On the house." Marianne produced two shot glasses, and she had them filled before they even landed on the bar. "We'll toast your good news."

Burl grabbed one of the glasses, staggering backwards as he raised it. "Let's hope this one's a girl." He placed the shot glass against his lips and sucked the liquid through the gaps in his teeth. Losing his balance, he grabbed the bar to right himself.

Marianne glanced down at his grazed hands and torn fingernails. One would be forgiven for thinking he'd been fighting, but Marianne knew better. Burl's nightly trips to the brothel began and ended with a clumsy climb through his bedroom window. She also knew that he and his overbearing wife hadn't shared a bedroom for some years, and that, according to her girls, he'd been incapable of any activity required to produce babies for quite some time. And so, if she was sure of one thing, it was that however Burl's wife had got pregnant, it wasn't by him.

Still, she smiled sweetly, and raised her own glass. "Here's to it being a girl." She drained the glass and slammed it down onto the bar. "You'll be a hero if it is."

Burl grabbed his crotch. "My wand's a magic one." He thrust his hips forward and staggered sideways, knocking over a bar stool. "Maybe you'll let me show you one day."

Marianne laughed lightly. "Maybe, Burl. Maybe." She glanced up at the ceiling above her and watched as the lights slightly swayed back and forth. "Will you excuse me?"

She swept out from behind the bar, the layers of sheer fabric she always wore sailing behind her like ghosts in her wake. As she reached the stairs she could hear feet running up and down the landing above.

As she made her way up, two men, half dressed, with shirts and trousers bundled into their fists, pushed past her and made for the exit. Marianne stopped and watched them leave. The only time she'd ever known patrons exit in such a hurry, was when their wives had appeared at the door looking for them.

She hurried up the rest of the stairs and found the landing in absolute chaos.

The Linden Tree was an unusually large house for Lynstock. While the other houses were crammed together, or had been separated into individual flats, if they were even big enough to be called that, the administration granted Marianne's business as much room as it needed. It kept the ever growing population of single men happy, and it protected the women on The Hope from being attacked or raped. While those women were reserved for arranged marriages, and a lifetime of breeding in the hope of producing a rare baby girl, Marianne's girls were all from the slums. The women the administration didn't care about.

The landing was a long hallway, lushly carpeted, with walls in a matching flock wallpaper, and heavy velvet drapes framing each bedroom door. Marianne had decorated the space with large paintings and side tables, vases of flowers and small statuettes. The Linden Tree was smart and clean, and a whole world away from the grubby little places on The Floor where men could go for a quick grope and leave with regrets that would have them itching for weeks. Marianne's girls were clean too. No drugs, no mental health issues, no diseases. She paid them well, and they took pride in themselves and their work.

But today, the landing looked like a crime scene. Tables had been toppled, paintings knocked askew, drapes tugged free from their rails. Marianne's girls ran from room to room, in various states of undress while white-faced men stood in the doorways, unsure of what to do.

"Gentlemen," Marianne called out, her voice sailing cleanly over the clamour of panic. "Please get dressed, make your way down to the bar and have some drinks on the house. I apologise for any inconvenience." She caught the eyes of some of her girls, sending them back into the bedrooms with a twitch of her head.

The men slowly made their way back downstairs. They were unsure, confused, curious, and Marianne found herself herding them like cattle.

When the floor was clear of men, Marianne clapped her hands and her girls appeared in their doorways. They all started talking at once, their shrill voices like budgies.

Marianne held up her hands. "Quiet."

Many of the faces that looked at her were streaked with mascara, their cheeks flushed, their eyes puffy. Somewhere, someone was crying. Wailing, in fact.

"What's happened up here?"

A line of arms were raised, pointing to an open

door further up the corridor.

Marianne walked towards it, stepping over broken vases and spilt flowers, and stopping to pick up toppled tables.

As she reached the door, some girls who were still gathered there stepped back like parting waters, their faces white, their hands clenched to their throats. Marianne glanced at her feet as she turned into the room, preparing herself for almost anything. Almost.

She could actually feel the blood draining from her face, flowing out of her hollowing chest, and pooling somewhere inside her legs. She gripped the door frame and screwed her eyes shut. Slowly opening them, she looked over the scene again, pressing her lips tightly together to contain the sob that threatened to escape them.

Hannah, one of her top girls, was lying in the oversized bath. She was wearing a silver sequined dress and her long blonde hair was loose, waving back and forth in the water. It was like looking at a mermaid. The effect would have been quite beautiful if her skin hadn't been so grey, so sallow. If her mouth hadn't been hanging slackly open. If her open eyes hadn't been so glazed and empty. And if the water hadn't been so red with blood, and if her wrists weren't sliced open.

"What happened?" Marianne demanded, her voice taut and strained.

The girls around her instinctively stepped back, looking down at their feet.

"Come on," Marianne snapped. "What the hell

happened?"

"We just found her," one girl said.

"We were all busy with clients."

"She was already dead when..."

As a group, the women withdrew again.

Marianne took one last look into the bathroom before pulling the door closed. "Who's her room mate?"

Marianne carefully paired the girls together; new arrivals shared rooms with more experienced girls. They looked after one another, and became close friends. They always had someone to talk to, to laugh with, to cry with. Whatever happened during the day, they had a confidante they could trust.

"It's Corinn," someone mumbled.

Marianne turned around, and the wailing that had been in the background—a sound almost lost under the chaos—came to the fore, leading her feet further along the corridor. She stumbled on a rucked mat, only then realising how much her legs were shaking.

The door frame was damp as she grabbed it. The room looked like the rest of the corridor; furniture overturned, curtains ripped from their hooks, make up spilt across the floor. Marianne could smell talcum powder.

In the corner, Corinn's fingers extended from the tight ball she had crushed herself into, clawing and fighting. A few other girls tried to restrain and comfort her. Their arms were raw with scratches, their hair pulled loose from pins and bands. They looked up and withdrew from the hysterical bundle, allowing Marianne to approach.

Corinn raised her head; her bloated eyes heavy with tears, her reddened nose streaming.

A shiver ran through Marianne, although it would be several days before she'd be able to understand why. But in that moment, all she had was her gut feeling. And her gut told her to get rid of Corinn. Before she killed again.

2

Maeve paused with her foot hovering just above the first step. She looked up at the doors in front of her, the pillars flanking them, and it all looked somehow smaller. It lacked the impressive grandeur she had once seen in it, it lacked presence.

Faith pulled at her hand impatiently, already standing on the step above.

"You lived here once upon a time," Maeve said to her.

The girl turned back. Her big green eyes were shaded by thick lashes, and a fringe of wispy hair bobbed as she blinked.

"I lived here?" she repeated, turning back to the vast doors ahead. "It's a castle."

"It is like a castle. Come on. Let me introduce you to Denver. He knew you when you were a baby, and he won't believe how big you are now."

Maeve bowed her head and pushed herself forward up the steps. She placed her hand on the cool door handle, twisted, and pushed the door open.

Maeve stopped in the doorway, blinking in the darkness inside. The sun was warm on her back while the cool, stale air inside raised goosebumps on her forearms. The space felt bigger, emptier, more cavernous. Like a huge mouth ready to swallow her. Faith's hand tightened its grip on hers, and her small body shuffled in against her legs.

As the dark interior came into focus, Maeve realised just how unfamiliar it had become. It still smelt the same—the dust, the papery smell of old books—but the mountains of books had disappeared, leaving the floor completely clear. The walls were lined with filled bookshelves, and more shelves created a labyrinth of aisles and walkways. As Maeve crept further inside, she could see neatly written labels on the shelves; the books carefully ordered into categories, and shelved by author.

"Can I help?"

Maeve jumped at the voice that echoed around her.

"Sorry, I didn't mean to—" Denver stopped, halfway across the shop floor. "My God." He folded his arms over his chest. "Hello stranger."

Maeve looked him up and down. If it was possible, he looked like he'd actually lost weight.

"Hello Denver."

Denver glanced down at Faith. "This can't be..." He walked over to them and crouched down, looking Faith over. "My God. She was just a little baby last time I saw her."

"She's three now," Maeve said. She crouched down and spoke to Faith. "This is Denver. Say hello."

Faith stepped forward, considering Denver closely. She reached out her hand and lay her white fingers over his brown forearm. She studied it for a moment, nodded, apparently satisfied, and withdrew her hand.

"Hello Denver," she said.

Denver looked up at Maeve. "I can't believe how much she's grown."

"And I can't believe this place. I guess you really were doing something with all those books after all."

Denver straightened up, arching his stiff back. "I told you all I knew what I was doing. You can find exactly what you want now. There's cooking sections, healthcare, children's books. Books about poison." Denver winked and Maeve turned away as her face flushed.

"Then there's the secondary business. After everyone abandoned me here, I had nothing to do with all the rooms in the back, so I rent them out now."

"To who?"

"Anyone who wants them. Prostitutes, healers, gamblers, social groups. I hire them out by the hour, no questions asked."

"Still dabbling in all things illegal then."

"Yep. Still risking my neck. Life just isn't exciting enough if I'm not." Denver smiled, but his eyes stayed sour. "So what are you up to these days, other than being a surrogate mother?"

"Helping at the refuge mostly. I'm also working

a few hours in a bar. I get all the clothes and toys that Faith needs from donations via the refuge, but I like to buy her some stuff that's just hers. Things no one else has worn or played with. She deserves that at least."

"Do you ever see anyone else? Kerise?" He frowned. "Tale?"

"We see a lot of Kerise." Maeve looked down at Faith who was tugging at her skirt. She bent and hefted her onto her hip. "Don't we sweetheart? Yeah, Kerise is around at least once a week. She often stays for supper. I haven't seen Tale at all though. I kept thinking I should pop round but, well, time just got away from us."

"I haven't seen anything of Kerise in almost two years, and I doubt Tale will ever speak to me again."

Maeve reached out and touched his arm. "None of that was your fault, you were just trying to help as best you could. I'd have done the same thing. She just needed someone to focus her anger on. A scapegoat."

Denver shrugged. "Maybe."

"Has there been any word from Freda at all?"

"I doubt we'll ever hear from her again."

Maeve lowered her voice. Some questions could only be asked in a whisper. "Do you think she's still alive?"

Denver cleared his throat and glanced up at the ceiling. "I have to believe she is. I have to believe it was all worth it."

"I'm sorry, Denver, I shouldn't have just

disappeared. I should have..." She drifted off. What could she have done? Fought to keep the resistance together? Acted as everyone's agony aunt? She had Faith to look after, she couldn't look after everyone else as well. But it hurt to see Denver so lost. He was little more than a ghost of himself.

"Don't fret over it." Denver smiled tightly and turned away, setting off at a brisk walk across the shop. "You have your own problems."

He stepped in behind the counter, and crouched down behind it. "Drink?" came his muffled voice.

"Yes please. Something cold. And some fruit juice for Faith if you have any."

Denver's hands appeared, placing three glasses on the counter.

Maeve settled Faith on a bar stool. She placed her hands on the girl's bony shoulders and looked her in the eye. "Sit still, and don't try to get down because it's too high, you'll fall and hurt yourself."

Faith smiled and nodded, glancing quickly at the drop to the floor. Maeve turned the stool towards the bar and eased it a little closer before levering herself up into the next seat.

Denver stood up with a bottle of fruit juice in his hand, and poured out three drinks. "Ice?"

"No thanks." Maeve picked up one of the glasses and drank half before placing it in front of Faith. "Both hands," she said as Faith reached for it. Maeve looked back at Denver and smiled.

"Proper little mother, aren't you?" Denver said.

Maeve beamed. "I'm trying to be. It's hard though. I barely remember my own mother, so I have no idea if I'm doing it right. I just wish I had someone to learn from."

Denver picked at an imaginary fleck on the bar. "Any news about your father yet?"

Maeve shook her head. "Nothing."

"And the refuge?"

"It's his legacy, and it's still helping as many women and children as it can. In fact, it's never been busier, we're struggling to cope. And, of course, we're always looking over our shoulders. I'm scared every day that they'll find her. Realise who she is."

Denver reached out and placed his hand over Maeve's. "He'd be really proud of you."

"I just wish we could have him back. He's really missed." She blinked, her eyes brimming. "I miss him."

3

Marianne was vaguely aware that someone was speaking to her, but as she leaned on the bar, a cloth in one hand, her other resting on the large knife she always kept under the counter, her attention was focussed elsewhere.

She watched Corinn waitressing. She walked around like all her joints were partly ceased, her eyes on the floor, hair over her face. Her mouth moved constantly, mumbling to herself as her eyes flicked from side to side. Marianne watched the clients shy from her, preferring to wait for another girl rather than let her serve them.

Lifting her eyes to the rest of the room, Marianne watched her other girls. They floated between the tables, smiling, chatting, flirting. They befriended everyone there, making it their business to know names, occupations, marital statuses. They listened, eavesdropped, and reported back to Marianne. She knew exactly which patrons might cause trouble before they even knew it themselves.

She turned her eyes back to Corinn. The girl

had stopped, mid-step, in the middle of the room. Her eyes were fixed on a man a few tables away from her. Marianne knew him well: Cole Hays, an importer and exporter from Haverhead. A regular customer. A wealthy customer. A valued one.

Marianne patted the bar, finally looking up at Burl who sat on the other side. He was still talking, but Marianne hadn't been listening for some time.

"Excuse me, Burl," she said, sweeping out from behind the bar. She strode across the room, smiling sweetly to the regulars who called out her name, side stepping those who approached her, keen to capture her in conversation.

She glanced around as someone grabbed her hand.

"Hey Marianne, where are you going in such a hurry?" He was a new customer, maybe not yet understanding the rules. But Marianne could feel the air prickle around her. The regulars would remind him of his place. They might have a quiet word with him, send him home with no more than a hurt sense of pride, or Marianne would be patching him up later. Either way, he'd learn not to touch any of the girls without invitation and a credit exchange.

Marianne smiled and pulled her hand from his damp fingers. "Always busy-busy," she said, keeping her voice as flat as she could.

People were moving around now; waitresses, customers. The dancers were changing shift and the bar was getting busy. Marianne craned her neck for a glimpse of Corinn. It took her a moment to spot her, and only a moment more to cross the room and grab her by the arm.

She pulled her away from Cole Hays. The sudden motion threw Corinn off balance and she tripped, pulling Marianne to the floor with her.

Cole stood up, smoothed down his suit, and grimaced at the torn pocket on his jacket.

"You want to keep your girls under control," he said. He glared at Corinn. "Or locked up in that one's case."

Marianne untangled herself from Corinn, and staggered up to standing.

"I'm so sorry, Cole. I'll pay for the damage. She's new, she's—"

"She's completely out of control," Cole interjected. He stepped forward and Marianne could feel his breath on her face. "She's your responsibility, and I suggest you get her sorted."

"Have your dog put down, Marianne," called a voice.

Ignoring it, Marianne followed Cole to the door. "I'm sorry, Cole, I'll sort it, I'll get rid of her."

"You better Marianne. I don't want to see that girl again. You know that I can get this whole place shut down like that." He clicked his fingers and Marianne flinched.

"I'm sorry," she repeated. She hated herself for grovelling, hated the whinging, desperate tone in her voice. She turned back towards the room, running her eyes over it. She'd do whatever it took to keep this place going, to keep her girls fed, housed, safe. And right now, what she needed to do was damage control.

For the second time in as many weeks Marianne called for free drinks at the bar. In her head, she imagined her profits pouring away like water.

Corinn was still sitting where she had fallen, half of her hidden beneath a table, her face hidden behind her hair. Her white fingers flicked back and forth as if she were debating heavily with someone.

Reaching out, Marianne touched Corinn's shoulder. Her head snapped up, and her dark eyes locked onto Marianne's.

"She cries, she cries, but she's always thinking," Corinn said, her fingers flicking against her temples. "She's going to kill him, and soon. She cries, but she's plotting, always plotting, always planning. She'll kill him with a broken pipe, she's been working on it, every night, every night when he leaves. Blood. Blood. She'll kill him."

Swallowing back the knot of fear tightening her throat, Marianne grabbed Corinn's arm and pulled her to her feet. She wrapped the girl's tiny frame against herself, and hurried her towards the stairs.

"She's just feeling a little under the weather," Marianne explained to curious patrons. "She just needs some rest."

And all the while, Corinn muttered. "She'll kill him. She'll kill him."

4

"What's going on?" asked Maeve.

The three sisters that worked in the refuge were pressed up against the window, their ample hips swaying in unison like an armada of warships.

They turned together, like some kind of three-headed creature.

"The administration are here," one of the heads said.

Maeve stiffened, and her eyes flicked towards the ceiling. "Here coming to the refuge?"

"Here on The Floor. There's several officers in the street. They look like they're going door to door."

"I need to get Faith out of here. If they find her —" Maeve couldn't bring herself to finish the sentence. She rushed to the window and pressed her cheek against the cool glass, straining her eyes up the street. The officers were still some way off.

"Do you think they've picked up the search for her again?" another sister asked. "We've not seen an officer down here for more than two years."

"Let's hope not."

Maeve took the stairs two at a time and skidded into the bedroom. She looked down at the sleeping child, and then glanced around the room. Every bed was occupied with a woman escaping something or someone, some with children of their own to look after.

Maeve shook Faith's shoulder gently. The girl stirred, her soft face creasing into a frown. She whimpered and screwed her fists into her eyes.

"Sorry to wake you, sweetheart, but it's time to go."

Faith whined and pushed Maeve away.

"Come on, Faith, we have to go now," Maeve snapped.

Faith sat up and began to cry, tears rolling over her cheeks. Maeve felt her face flush as the other women turned to stare.

"Come on, poor thing's still half asleep," one of them said.

"What's the panic?" asked another.

Maeve opened her mouth to warn them of what was coming, but then clamped it shut again. The last thing the sisters needed was a stampede. Besides, if the officers were looking for Faith, the other women had nothing to worry about.

Maeve lifted Faith onto her hip and scooped up her bag with the other hand. With her heart pounding she hurried down the stairs, instinctively avoiding any places the old wood cracked or squeaked. She doubted that she'd ever lose that old habit.

Because the refuge was built right against the cliff, they didn't have the advantage of a back door. Maeve had to take Faith out the front, right into the path of the approaching officers.

"Go, Maeve, Go!" said the three-headed creature at the window. "They're almost here."

Maeve grabbed the door handle, but her sweaty hand slipped straight off. She wiped her hand on her dress and tried again, this time managing to swing the door open. The small bell above the door jingled, and a chill went through Maeve's insides. It was another habit she doubted she'd lose.

Out in the air of the slums, the gentle stench of the river was trapped below the sagging canopy of clouds. Faith wrinkled her nose and pressed her face into Maeve's neck.

Maeve glanced up the road. A group of officers, guns strapped to their hips, were working their way down both sides of the street. Women and children leaned out of windows, men hung out of doorways, watching the progression of the uniforms through the slums. It wasn't just an unusual sight, it was unheard of, and wholly unwelcome.

Following the march of the officers, there was an even larger force of locals. They followed closely, and placed themselves in front of every door the officers knocked on. But what struck Maeve as really odd, was that the officers weren't retaliating. They were being forcibly turned away from every door, yet they simply made a mark on their tablets and moved on.

But Maeve didn't have time to watch the proceedings, the officers were just a couple of doors away from the refuge. Hitching Faith further up onto her hip, Maeve hurried down the steps to the street. Balancing along the wooden boards that acted as makeshift walkways, She pushed her way into Downstride.

The street was filled with people, their voices thickening the air. They wandered—deep in conversation, and calling their neighbours to follow them—towards The Wall, while Maeve tried to find a pathway through them.

She dodged back and forth, ducking under some elbows, bouncing off others. She gripped Faith harder, and the girl buried her face into Maeve's shoulder.

"It's alright," Maeve whispered to her, "just hold on tight. Not far now."

By the time Maeve reached the river, the crowd had thinned to just a few people; those too busy or uncaring to follow the masses without knowing what they were doing. At the river's edge, some had abandoned their work, leaving pitchforks sticking up out of the silt like winter trees, but most simply continued with their labour. Most couldn't afford not to.

"What's all that about?" one man asked her, tipping his cap back with a dirty wrist.

"There's officers on The Wall. They're going house to house."

The man grunted. "Looking for spare women

no doubt."

Maeve shook her head. "They can't be. They've never taken from the slums before. They can't." Faith squeaked as Maeve squeezed her tighter.

"If they're running out of women, what else can they do? We've got no problem producing girls down here." He pulled off his hat and rubbed his face with it. "They'll be marrying our girls off soon enough, just you wait."

Maeve looked back towards The Wall. She could only hope it wasn't true.

5

Kerise listened as a series of heavy bolts were drawn back, and thick chains unhooked. There were thirteen in all, Kerise had stood here and counted them before. She stepped back out of the doorway and glanced quickly up and down the street as the last bolt was drawn back.

The door was barely open a crack before Kerise pushed her way inside.

Marianne's hand clamped around Kerise's wrist. "You nearly knocked me flying!" she said.

Kerise pulled Marianne back upright and pushed the door shut.

"I'm sorry, I just don't want to be seen out on the street."

Marianne brushed back her hair and smoothed down her clothes; realigning the numerous layers of chiffon and lace. She was like an entire wardrobe in one woman.

"I guess I should have made sure the back door was open for you," Marianne said.

Kerise grinned. "Maybe you should." She stepped aside as Marianne set about relocking the front door. "What did you want me for?"

"First, a drink. What can I get you?"

"Just a water will be fine."

"Typical Kerise." Marianne led the way through a heavy velvet curtain into the large lounge beyond, and swept in behind the bar. She poured a large glass of water for Kerise, and a small sherry for herself.

Kerise glanced around the room—heavy leather seats, thick carpets, large portraits covering the walls—and eased herself onto a bar stool. She always found it hard to breathe in here; like the thick furnishings and fabrics were trying to drown her.

She took three big gulps of her drink, almost choking on it. Even the water here was too plush and heavy.

"What can I do for you Marianne?" Kerise asked. She was eager to get business done and back out in the fresh air. It smelled too much like male drool in here.

Marianne leaned over the counter. "I need you to take someone for me."

"Take someone?"

"One of my girls. She's new, but it's not really working out."

Kerise frowned. "For one thing, what do you mean 'take'? What, dispose of? Relocate to a nice condo in the suburbs? And for another, when do you ever get rid of your girls? They're like family to you. What the hell has this girl done?"

Marianne sighed and flexed her hands. "I mean take away. Just take her somewhere else. Somewhere safe. But somewhere away from here."

"What did she do?"

Despite the bar being empty, Marianne glanced around before replying in a whisper. "She's a psychic."

Kerise gripped hold of her stool. "What you're asking me to do—"

"I know, I know," Marianne interrupted. "If I had any other options... I didn't know who else to turn to. It's not like I could take out an ad in the paper. I just need her out of here. She's been saying things, doing things. She's scaring off my customers, and my girls are really spooked. I can't have her here. She's too dangerous."

"She'll be dangerous wherever she is. Why should I burden someone else with that kind of risk? Why should I burden myself?"

Marianne shook her head. "You shouldn't. I just didn't know what else to do."

Kerise folded her arms and chewed her bottom lip. This would be a very big favour. "Where did she come from?"

"That's the really curious thing. I can't even remember. I'm not even sure when she arrived here. You know how carefully I keep track of my girls, how carefully I recruit them. But Corinn... One day she wasn't here, and the next day she was. I honestly can't give a better explanation than that."

Kerise shook her head. "I've got so many

warning bells going off here."

"I wish I could give you more assurances."

"So do I." Kerise drummed her fingers on the bar. "I'll tell you what, let me see if I can secure a spot for her first. If I can't find anyone willing to take her, she's your problem."

"That's fair."

"And if I do manage to find somewhere, you will owe me the biggest favour you've ever owed anyone in your life."

6

Marianne didn't often leave her business, but after that morning's conversation with Kerise, she couldn't get Corinn off her mind. In fact, her head had filled up with all manner of frightening visions. She needed some fresh air.

Normally, when Marianne needed to clear her head, she would head to a small, shady park at the far end of Duties. It was always quiet and rarely visited by anyone else. Everyone on Lynstock worked, and they worked hard, using labour to keep their demons at bay. The single men worked to forget that they were single and that, in all likelihood, always would be. The married men worked to forget the fact that they had failed to produce a daughter, and women worked to forget that they were no more than breeding machines with little hope of fulfilling their ultimate purpose. Lynstock was not a happy place, and so, the few parks were always peaceful.

As it happened, Marianne didn't go to her favourite park today. In an uncharacteristic change of heart, Marianne turned in the other direction and followed Silk Lane towards the steps up to Haverhead. She'd never be able to explain why, or at least, with no more of a satisfactory answer than 'that's just where my feet wanted to go'.

Stopping at the bottom of the steps, Marianne looked up them towards Haverhead. As a girl born in the slums, even gazing upon this level of the city had once been nothing but a dream. But here she was, her hand gripped around the banister, and her feet lifting her up step by step.

Few people made their way up to Haverhead in the morning. Men trundled down the steps in their suits to oversee the work of their Lynstock employees, and it would be several hours before they made their way back up again, satisfied after a good day of business. They'd kiss their wives, pat their sons on their heads, and, if they were fortunate enough, hug their daughters. They'd settle down to a cooked meal, served by domestics, and have not a worry in the world. Not the worries of their employees, making their way back to their homes and the inescapable realities of their lives.

As Marianne reached the top of the steps, her feet carried her along The Lawns. The houses here boasted long, sweeping gardens, manicured with striped lawns, rose bushes, and only the tidiest and most docile of shrubs. Nothing unruly, nothing that would dare sprout up where it wasn't wanted.

At the far end of The Lawns, an ambulance was parked on the road. The lights on its roof spun lazily, throwing blue lights in a repetitive arc across the buildings. The back doors were open, but the paramedics were busy speaking to administration officers, rather than attending to the body inside. It could only be that a body was all that it was.

Marianne wandered towards the scene, her curiosity outweighing the instinctive urge to turn around, an instinct she hadn't quite managed to shrug off from her slum days. But Marianne had the freedom of the city now. Not only were many of the officers and their superiors customers of hers—a fact she remained discreet about—but she paid a hefty licence fee to the administration every month. Of course, there was no such thing as a licensed brothel, it was simply that her 'bar' paid several times more than the usual rate.

One of the officers looked up and nodded to her. She'd seen him at The Linden Tree before.

"What's going on?" She wasn't afraid to be brazen; there were few officers that would dare to tell her to mind her own business. With the city's rich and powerful counted amongst her loyal clientèle, most of what happened in Falside was her business.

"One of yours, I think: Cole Hays."

Marianne stumbled. "Cole?"

"Know him well did you?"

"He's dead? How?" She glanced towards the back of the ambulance.

"Murder," the officer confirmed.

"Do you know who?"

The officer stepped closer and lowered his voice. "Quite the scandal actually. Turns out the dirty old bugger had some kind of dungeon built into his cellar. Had three girls living down there. Slum girls, no tracking on them. Using them, you know, for his pleasures. Kinky old git as well apparently. I've not seen it myself, but the guys say he's got quite the set up down there. Liked to..." he glanced around him, "cut them. You know?"

Marianne nodded and looked back at the ambulance. Yes, she knew.

"Anyway, one of them had been working an old pipe loose. Hit him round the back of his head with a force that almost pushed his brain out through his eye sockets. He never saw it coming." He grinned; all teeth.

"What's going to happen to the girls?"

"At the moment, we've got them doped up on tranquillisers. They're like savage animals. God knows what we'll do with them. They'll probably spend the rest of their days under lock and key."

"After they've suffered so much already."

The officer shrugged. "Not much left there to rehabilitate." He tapped his forehead.

Marianne stared up at the house. "And the neighbours didn't hear anything?"

"Amazing isn't it. The wife claims even she didn't know." He turned and looked at the house himself. "You can't even imagine the things that go on behind locked doors." He turned back to Marianne. "Even the respectable ones. Anyway, what brings you up to Haverhead?"

Marianne shook her head. "I have to go."

7

The sister creature moved to the door, filling the space with six huge breasts before the officer made it all the way up the stairs.

In the rooms above them they had seven terrified women, and three terrified children. They were not about to let in a man simply because he had a uniform and a list of addresses.

The officer reached the top of the steps, still frowning at his screen. He was a young man; looked barely out of school, with patches of facial hair that didn't require daily shaving yet. He finally looked up, and his mouth fell open as his eyes roved back and forth over the sisters. He swallowed hard, his throat bobbing up and down like a fishing float.

"Madam?" he offered.

"What do you want?" snapped one of the sisters.

The officer referred back to his screen for a prompt.

"I have been instructed by the administration to

conduct a census of all persons residing on The Floor. Please allow me access to your building and bring all residents and visitors to the ground floor for registration."

"No," said the sisters. In unison, they folded their arms, creating an impenetrable barrier of flesh.

"Wh—what?" The officer scrolled through his screen for help.

"You won't find the answer there. Now get lost."

"But you're required by law—"

"By whose law?" One of the sisters stepped forward, birthing herself from the other two. "Your laws don't mean diddly-squat down here. You're out of your jurisdiction, son. We pay taxes to the slum authorities, not to you. Those taxes are distributed to the people, not used to line the pockets of those with enough lining already. We don't benefit from your administration, so we don't have to answer to it. Falside stops at the steps, son. Now get out of here."

The officer opened and closed his mouth a few times before flushing bright red and trundling away down the steps.

Satisfied, the sister creature moved back inside, slapping its hands together with satisfaction.

"That did it," one said.

"He won't be back."

"Give a boy a uniform, and he thinks—" The sentiment had to be left unfinished as someone hammered at the door. The bell above it rang back and forth with the impact.

"Well that's not some jumped up little kid."

The sisters moved back to the door, fortifying themselves before opening it.

They couldn't help but nod in approval at the man stood before them. His shoes reflected their open mouths, his buttons mirrored their wide eyes over and over, and he had so many stripes on his shoulders they were almost tumbling down his arms. His face was weathered, with a sizeable scar along his chin, and as he removed his hat, his silver hair glimmered in the sunlight. He smiled and tipped his head.

"Ladies."

The sisters babbled, unable to construct a single sentence between them.

"I am Captain Rush. My officer informs me that there's been a misunderstanding here. I can only apologise. We're not here to force ourselves into buildings and register people at gunpoint. Let me explain what we are hoping to accomplish.

"It has come to the attention of the administration that The Floor has been left completely overlooked. While the citizens of Falside are benefiting from advancements in housing, utilities, technology, security, and healthcare, we've been failing everyone on The Floor by denying them access to such things.

"We are here to address that failing. We're simply counting people, nothing more than that, so that we can give everyone access to much needed services and resources. So, your assistance in this matter would be much appreciated."

The sisters giggled and jostled one another; flesh jiggled. Somehow, while the captain had been talking, they'd all moved inside. The sisters looked around, surprised, not sure how it had happened.

"Now, ladies," the captain continued, "if you could gather everyone in the building down here, we can begin registration.

"I'm not sure about this," one of the sisters said.

"This is a refuge. The women here are vulnerable, scared."

"Exactly what does this registration entail?"

"Just a few details," the captain said. He pulled a slim metal band from his pocket. "Each woman will be issued with an ID bracelet so that they can access healthcare on The Hope. Regular check ups, screening, vitamins, maternity services. It's for their own good."

One of the sisters stepped forward and took the band from the captain. She held it up and inspected it, turning it this way and that. It looked like nothing more than an innocuous hinged circle of lightweight metal.

"And they have to wear these?"

"Once they're fitted, they can't be removed. It prevents people swapping bracelets. It helps us to ensure the services are provided to those most in need."

Another sister took the bracelet and looked it over. "He's good at making it sound like it's all for our benefit, isn't he?"

The third sister took it. "No doubt this will be tracking them wherever they go."

The captain cleared his throat. "The doorways of health centres and service providers will be the only doorways tracking these ID bracelets, simply so that we can refine the services on offer. Make them more useful to the women that need them."

The sisters looked at one another. "Marketing," they all agreed.

The third sister handed the bracelet back. "Sorry, Captain, it was a nice spiel and we especially liked the packaging," she looked him up and down, "but we're not interested."

Captain Rush smiled. "I don't think you're quite understanding this, ladies."

"I think we're understanding just fine. The administration is running out of women and wants to start stealing them from the slums instead. The women it has always ignored, shunned. Suddenly it needs them. This is all just sugar coating."

"No, you're not. You see, this isn't a decision. This isn't your choice. You will bring downstairs anyone in this building, or we will fetch them ourselves at gunpoint."

"There are children here."

"Then I'm sure you don't want to turn this into something it doesn't need to be."

Captain Rush crossed the café and opened the door. He clicked his fingers and half a dozen armed officers entered.

"So why don't you go and get everyone together, and we can start the registration process."

8

Kerise looked up at the small window. She placed one foot on the crate that still stood on the ground. It cracked and pitched under her weight, ripping free from some of the weeds entangling it. Kerise grabbed the window ledge, pushing the window a little further open. As she pulled herself up into the gap, she wondered if Denver had simply forgotten to shut the window, or if he still hoped Tale might return.

Inside, the room had been cleared of the old boxes and stacked papers it had once hoarded. Instead, a table sat at its centre, surrounded by too many chairs. Below the window, a sofa was positioned to catch Kerise.

The corridor beyond was empty, but men's voices were gathered somewhere, behind one of the closed doors.

Kerise stopped outside one. Tale's office. She touched the door handle and an avalanche of memories tumbled through her brain. She snatched her hand away, and shook her head, trying to clear the snowfall of thoughts. But some clung like slush, gathered in the gutters and sheltered corners. She laid her hand on the handle again, turned it, and pushed the door open.

The smell hit her first; that familiar breath of electricity, of warm machine parts, of brewing coffee. She squinted, and almost thought she saw Tale sat at her desk. Her oversized glasses, a steaming mug in her hand, a scowl to hide the smile underneath. And Freda, red hair catching the light, long legs elegantly crossed, her eyes never wavering from the woman she loved.

The room was exactly how Tale had left it. Kerise sat in Tale's chair and lay her hands over the keyboard in front of her. Two large boxes were stacked under the desk; unopened mail addressed to Asteria. Denver was just waiting for the day she came back.

Kerise stood, backed out of the room, and gently closed the door.

"Hello stranger," she said. She turned round and nodded at Denver who leaned casually against the wall.

"No one can ever sneak up on you, can they?"

Kerise tried to smile, but her face felt tight and unfamiliar.

Denver straightened. "Where've you been, Kerise?"

"Around, you know. I'm always around."

"No, you haven't been. I've not laid eyes on you in two years. I've not seen anyone. Well,

Maeve dropped by the other day, with Faith. But then, you'll probably know that. I hear you two see quite a lot of each other."

"She needs me."

"And I don't? For three years I've languished here by myself. Tale hasn't said one word to me, I haven't even seen her, Freda could be dead for all we know, I may as well be dead to my own family, and Maeve returned to the slums with Faith. Everyone I ever thought I could trust has abandoned me. But now here you are, no doubt to ask me some massive favour." He folded his arms. "Well? Let's hear it."

Kerise looked at her boots, running her eyes over the scuffed toes. She needed new ones, but she hadn't worked in months, and her pockets were beginning to get a little light.

"I'm not your keeper, Denver. I don't owe anyone anything."

"Oh yes, how could I forget. Kerise is a lone wolf. Don't ask her where she's going or where she's been. Don't ask about her past. Don't get close, and don't expect anything in return." Denver turned and marched up the corridor.

Kerise hurried after him. "Alright, alright, I'm sorry. Is that what you want to hear? I should have checked on you. Made sure you were doing ok."

Denver stopped. "I didn't want you to check on me, Kerise. I wanted you to care."

"I'm sorry. I don't know what more to say. But I was hurting too. Everything I do is to protect Falside's women. I keep them safe, I break the law to protect them, I put myself in harm's way, and for what? For Freda to sneak out of the city, Tale to disappear into the system, and for the very heart to fall out of the resistance. And I find myself wondering why I bothered at all."

"So my penis is the problem?"

Kerise threw her hands into the air. "Oh, Denver! I'm not your personal guard, I'm not anyone's. I have my own demons to wrestle with, and those demons have been very vocal these last few years. Did you ever think about what I might have needed? Maybe I needed you to care. If you had visited Maeve and Faith you'd have easily found me, but you never did. You holed yourself up in here with your books and cried self pity. Ok, so no one came to see you, but you didn't go to see anyone else either."

Denver's eyes flooded with tears as he dropped his focus to the floor. "I guess we all got a bit wrapped up with our own demons then."

"We've all let each other down."

"Freda would never forgive us." Denver looked back at Kerise. "Do you think she's alive?"

"I think Freda's one of the most resourceful and capable women I know."

"I wonder if we'll ever see her again."

Kerise shrugged. "All we can do is hope."

Denver nodded slowly. "So, let's get to it, what's the favour you came to ask me?"

"I need to hide someone here for a while."

"Not another baby."

Kerise smiled. "Don't worry, this one's toilet

trained. But, she's also a psychic."

"No. No way, I can't have her."

"Come on, Denver, it's only until I find something a little more permanent for her."

Denver raised his hands in resignation. "Seriously, I just can't. I get a lot of officers in here, captains even, people high up in the administration. It's just way too dangerous."

Kerise raised her eyebrows. "You really do have quite the clientèle. But, I understand. I'll look for somewhere else for her."

"I'm sorry."

"That's alright, but I might make use of you again yet."

"I'll leave the window open for you."

Kerise grinned and awkwardly patted Denver on the shoulder. It was as close to a hug that he'd ever get from her. "I'll see you around then."

"I'll hold you to that."

9

Marianne closed the door to her office. She'd managed to avoid engaging in a conversation of more than a few snipped words all morning, and all she wanted was to get through the rest of the day in the same way. The girls could manage themselves for one day, and the patrons would simply have to do without her.

Marianne's office was small; she didn't need much space for herself. Having grown up sharing a single bedroom with three sisters and a baby brother, she wouldn't know what to do with large amounts of space.

The tightly buttoned leather of her chaise longue creaked under her as she settled into its curve. It wasn't particularly comfortable, but it fitted the impression she wanted people to have of her. Tucked underneath it, out of sight, was a simple camp bed which she used each night. But the smell of the leather was comforting, the feel of it, just having it near. It reminded her of how far she'd come, and how much she never wanted to go back.

A light knock on the door roused her from her thoughts and forced her eyes into a roll. She lay back and rested her arm across her forehead.

"Come," she called.

The door opened and, whoever it was coming in, stepped onto the thick carpet, their footsteps swallowed into the fibres. The door closed behind them. The room was silent.

"Well, what is it? My head is throbbing." Marianne waved her free hand at the intruder. She waited. "Well, if you're not going to speak, just leave me in peace."

"Look at me, Marianne."

Marianne couldn't put a face to the voice. "I can't. The lights."

"You're not ill. You're a liar. Just like little Mattie Kennett. Isn't that right? He's a little liar too, isn't he?"

Marianne jolted upright, hitting her elbow on the arm of the chaise. She blinked and stared at Corinn.

Gripping the edge of the chaise, she tested her dried out mouth. "Wh—wh—where did you hear that name?"

Corinn smiled. "Poor little Mattie. You never did find out what his father did to him, but you never saw him again, did you?"

"G—get out." Marianne wiped away sweat snaking over her temple.

Corinn laughed lightly and skipped over to Marianne. She settled herself on the other end of the chaise and crossed her legs up onto the leather. Reaching out, she grabbed Marianne's hands in hers.

"Don't worry about that, I came to ask you something else." She chattered happily, like they were childhood friends sharing secrets about the boys they liked. "Did you enjoy your walk this morning?"

"My walk?"

"I always think it's nice to try out new places, see new things. Better than going to the same boring park every time. So, did you enjoy where I sent you?"

"You?"

"Oh, Marri, try to keep up." She leant forward and tucked Marianne's hair behind her ear.

"How could you—"

Corinn laid her finger over Marianne's lips. "Don't ask the hows or the whys. I just wanted you to know what I *could* do."

"You knew that girl was going to..."

Corinn shook her head. "Nope. She was a pathetic little thing, she would never have had the balls to do anything like that. Not without a little help, at least."

"You?"

"Oh, Marri, catching on at last." She leaned forward and whispered into Marianne's ear. "I can do anything I want to." She kissed Marianne's cheek before leaning back again. "You want to get rid of me."

"No, I—"

"It's alright, I understand. Besides, a change of

scenery might be fun. More games to play."

"Games?" Marianne finally regained some control over her body, and backed away from Corinn, balling herself at the other end of the chaise. "People are dead. You're a murderer. You killed Hannah."

Corinn tilted her head side to side, weighing up the question. "Technically, Hannah killed herself. And technically, that girl killed Cole. I never held a knife or a broken pipe in my own hands."

"But you made them do it."

Corinn shrugged. "True, but only because they were so weak-willed."

"What do you want from me?"

Corinn lolled her head backwards. "Why would you ask me that? How boring. How predictable. You think you're that important that this is somehow all about you? I don't want anything from you Marri. Nothing at all."

"So why do it? Why show me what you're capable of?"

"Because it's fun. And because I'm bored."

"You killed them because you're bored?"

Corinn shrugged and stood up. "Why else would I do it?"

10

Maeve inspected the bracelet closely. It fit snugly to the wrist, so there was no way to look at the inside of it.

"Well, there's not much to know just by looking at it, is there? And it's just women being given one?"

"Any females over the age of fourteen," one of the sisters confirmed.

Maeve leaned back in her chair and glanced over at Faith. She was sat at a table by the window, removing flowers from a small vase and laying them out on the tablecloth.

"And what about the other children?" she asked.

"They're registered as their mother's dependants, so that they can access services on The Hope too. I suspect they felt sticking these on children would cause too much outcry."

"And the men?"

"The captain said that would be a development for the future."

"Which is unlikely," said another sister. She scratched at her wrist where the band sat against her skin. "They're doing to slum girls what they do to girls on The Hope. They'll be marrying them all off soon enough."

"Good luck marrying any of us off!" The three sisters laughed and shook against one another, but there was a heaviness to their laugh; like velvet drapes concealing a hidden room.

Maeve rubbed her own wrist, running her thumb over the tattooed line. "Is there anything we can do to stop them?"

The sisters shook their heads. "They came with guns."

Maeve looked back at Faith, and a solid rock of fear formed deep inside her belly. She had never missed her mother so much as she did in that moment.

"Then how can I possibly keep them away from Faith? They cannot find out who she really is, otherwise we're all dead."

11

Kerise always took the back entrance into The Linden Tree during business hours; a concealed entranceway that led into a narrow corridor. The walls were undecorated, and the bare wooden floor was neither polished nor even. But it was a convenient escape route for any customers whose wives came in the front door looking for them.

Kerise moved past Marianne's office towards the bar. Then she stopped and turned back.

A strip of light showed beneath the closed door, and a shadow passed back and forth, back and forth.

Kerise knocked. The pacing inside stopped, but there was no invitation to enter. Kerise knocked again.

"Marianne? It's Kerise."

Kerise was leaning slightly against the door, and almost fell as it suddenly opened. Marianne ushered her in and closed them into the small room.

"Are you alright?" Kerise asked. "You look like

you've hardly slept."

The woman, who usually presented as immaculate at any time of day or night, was far from her usual self. Her hair was escaping from its clips in loops and clumps, her make up was smeared, her cheeks hollow and pale, and dark crescents hung beneath her eyes. As she placed her glass on her desk, her hand shook.

"What's happened?"

Marianne raised a finger, the nail chewed back, and pointed towards the door. "You've got to take her. I need her gone."

Kerise took hold of Marianne's shoulders and eased her down onto the chaise longue. "You need to calm down. Take a deep breath, and tell me what's happened."

"She knows things, about everyone. She can do things. She's like no psychic I've ever met. Kerise, she's powerful, and she's evil. I don't care what you do with her, kill her for all I care, I just need her gone."

"Hey, slow down. What do you mean, she can do things?"

Marianne shook her head, her hair falling even looser.

"If I'm expected to take this girl away from you, I need to know what I'm dealing with. Always know what you're going into. And if you're right about her, this is huge, Marianne. I'm not going to kill her."

Marianne took a deep, ragged breath before exhaling slowly between smudged lips.

"She can control people. Make them do things.

Make them kill."

Kerise shook her head. "There's never been any talk of those sort of powers before."

"Then perhaps she's the first, I don't know, but she admitted it to me. And she admitted that she simply does it for entertainment."

"That can't be right. Perhaps you misunderstood."

Marianne pushed Kerise away and heaved herself to her feet. She made her way, unsteadily, to her desk and poured herself a large drink. With a shaking hand, she lifted the glass and drank its contents without stopping for breath.

"I did *not* misunderstand."

"I can see how scared you are, but you need to sleep, and you need to lay off the drink. You're obviously not thinking clearly. Let me talk to the girl. I'll make my decision then. But if she's as dangerous as you say she is, I can't imagine anyone wanting to take her in."

"She cannot stay here. If you can't take her, I'll hand her in to the administration."

Kerise stood. "I can only hope you didn't mean that."

"I did. I did mean it. I have to be loyal to my girls, to protect them. Screw loyalties to any other women. If you can't get rid of her, I'll have to get rid of her myself. No matter what that means."

"You are out of your bloody mind. I'll take the damn girl, and I'll speak to you when you're more rational." Kerise stormed over to the door and yanked it open. "And sober."

Kerise was directed to a bedroom upstairs, but none of the women would go near the room themselves. They cowered together, several feet away, babbling and whispering.

Kerise shook her head. Whatever kind of hysteria had got into Marianne, it was spreading like flu.

Corinn was huddled in the far corner of the room, her bony form wrapped up like a snake ready to strike. Kerise shook the thought from her mind. That hysteria really was catching. She crouched down and tried out the most reassuring smile she had.

"Hi. You must be Corinn. I'm Kerise. I've got somewhere safe to take you. You can trust me."

She reached out her hand, but Corinn shied away.

"You can trust me," Kerise repeated.

"Marianne said that," whispered Corinn. Kerise had to shuffle closer to hear her.

"I know. But things will be different this time, I promise."

"The girls say things about me. I can hear them. They whisper and whisper. They say I killed Hannah, but how could I? She killed herself. She was so sad. She told me. They were turning on her too." She rubbed her eyes. "She was getting older, and the younger girls wanted her out. They didn't like her having first pick of the customers. Said she didn't deserve it any more. They hated her. Just like they hate me."

"You're special, Corinn. And sometimes people

are scared of that."

"I'm scared of it too. Sometimes I hear them say things without it coming out of their mouth. I don't know how, it just comes into my head. Other things too. Memories, feelings. They get all crowded and I have to say them out loud to shut them up. Then everyone gets really angry at me. I wish I wasn't this way." She looked up as tears flowed down her face. "Why can't I just be normal?"

"Believe me, you wouldn't want to be. Let's get you out of here. Do you have anything to pack?"

Corinn shook her head.

Kerise held out her hand. "Come on then, let's get you somewhere safe."

As Corinn took hold of it, her eyes widened. "You miss her, don't you."

Kerise froze. "Miss who?"

Smiling, Corinn replied "Well, all of them."

12

Kerise slowly pushed the door open, jumping at the sound of the little bell that sung out above her head. A few women looked up from their drinks, but paid her little notice. She squeezed Corinn's hand and led her inside.

Three women were pressed in behind the counter, so tightly packed that it was impossible to tell where one ended and the next began.

Kerise snaked her way between the tables and led Corinn towards them.

"I'm wondering if you have space here for someone," Kerise enquired.

A thick hand was placed on the counter and one of the faces said "Of course, we never turn anyone away when they need a bed."

Kerise couldn't tell if the hand and the voice belonged to the same person.

"Would you like to come through?" One of the women peeled herself away from the other two, and her wide hips swayed their way down the hallway to the kitchen at the back of the house.

Kerise found herself feeling a little seasick from the motion.

In the kitchen, they all sat around the table, and for a moment they just looked at each other expectantly.

"Tell me a little about yourself," the woman finally said, addressing Kerise.

"The bed's not for me. It's for Corinn." She gestured. "I've brought her down from The Linden Tree. She's had some problems fitting in there. Corinn's quite a powerful psychic, so I'm sure that you can understand the need to keep her safe."

The woman's eyes widened in the flab of her face. "A psychic." She shook her head. "This is something way above my head. If only Father Harris were here. But, like I said, we don't turn away anyone in need."

"Thank you," Corinn muttered.

"But I think I'd like to speak to Maeve. That's Father Harris' daughter."

"I know," said Kerise. "I'm Kerise. I'm sure you'll have heard my name."

If it were possible, the woman's eyes widened even further. "Kerise! I'm so sorry for not recognising you, although how could I, we've never met, have we? We've never met."

"No, no, we've never met."

"My goodness, you look even tougher than I imagined you. Well, of course we'll take in Corinn, but I will bring Maeve in. I feel she'll be able to offer some insight the rest of us can't. But I will warn you; the administration are crawling all over the slums at the moment registering women. I don't know if we can keep Corinn hidden forever."

"I know you'll do your best."

"We will, we will. Oh, Kerise, bless you."

The woman reached out and smothered Kerise's hand inside both of hers. They were clammy and squashy, like over ripened fruit. Kerise slid her hand free.

"Then I'll leave her with you. Tell Maeve I'll be back soon to see her." Kerise turned to Corinn. "You'll be safe here, and well looked after, but with the administration around you need to keep your head down. Try not to draw too much attention to yourself. Do you understand?"

Corinn nodded.

"I'll come by in a few days to see how you're settling in. And you'll meet Maeve soon. She's very sweet, and her mother was...is a psychic, so I'm sure you two will get on well."

Corinn smiled. "Thank you Kerise. I'm sure me and Maeve will have lots of fun."

13

Dropping silently from the roof, Kerise steadied herself on top of the narrow wall, and crouched down. She enjoyed the feeling of watching someone while they remained oblivious to her presence.

She picked a loose chip of concrete from the top of the wall and threw it at the back of her brother's head.

He spun around, his body coiled and ready to fight. He looked left and right with a look of confusion before finally raising his eyes to where Kerise was balanced.

"I should've known it'd be you."

Kerise jumped down. "You should've, but you didn't. You're losing your touch, Tarin."

Tarin pulled Kerise into a tight embrace. "I'm getting old. The years have gone by and I've heard nothing from you since the last clean-up we did." He moved her out to arm's length. "You haven't got another one for me, have you?"

"No, this is just a personal visit."

Tarin frowned. "Why is it that I don't believe you? I see nothing of you for years, and then you turn up here just for a chin wag? Seems suspicious."

"Ok, ok, I do have something to ask you."

Tarin groaned and rolled his eyes.

Kerise raised her hands defensively. "It's just advice I'm after. That's all."

"Well in that case, I'm all yours. Want to come inside?"

"Am I welcome? I wouldn't want to upset the missus."

"You let me deal with Lucille. You're my little sister, you're always welcome."

Kerise followed Tarin inside, but as she crossed the threshold, she felt her shoulders tighten. This was her sister-in-law's domain, and despite her brother's protestations, Kerise knew that she was far from welcome here.

They settled themselves in the small, dark kitchen. Despite its modest size, every surface was crammed with cooking utensils, oven trays, mixing bowls, and several things Kerise couldn't even imagine the purpose of. Every spare wall was adorned with pots and pans, knives, wooden spoons strung together. There was meat hung; pheasants, rabbits, something that looked a lot like a squirrel. There were herbs and other plants, hanging baskets laden with fruit and vegetables. Anyone would think Lucille was a fine cook with a love of food, but in reality, she cooked like she was beating the food to death, and it usually tasted like it too. And a closer inspection of the kitchen would reveal mould, fungus, nests of silverfish, food crawling with flies and most likely maggots too.

"Can I get you something to eat?" Tarin offered.

Kerise shook her head.

"No, perhaps not. A drink then?"

"Just water, thanks." Kerise picked at a chip on the rim of the dirty serving bowl in front of her. "It amazes me that you're still alive eating from this kitchen."

Tarin patted his broad stomach. "Built like an ox, me. Good thing too."

"Well I hope the boys inherited your immunity."

"Luckily they did." Tarin placed a glass of water in front of Kerise. He sat down opposite. "So what can I do for you?"

"I've been thinking a lot," Kerise said.

"Uh oh."

She shot Tarin a glare. "Would you stop it? I don't even know where to start."

"Try the beginning."

"Alright, genius." Kerise took a deep breath. "After you cleaned up that room for me, everything fell apart. The resistance. Freda escaped the city and Tale disappeared into the system. She's not speaking to any of us. I just kind of withdrew. I've not done a single job in ages. It just seems so pointless. I don't even know what I'm fighting for anymore."

"Why didn't you come to me?"

"I didn't want to see anyone, not for a long

time. But then I started helping Maeve with Faith. I look after her sometimes when Maeve goes to work, or when she's needed at the refuge. It's been nice. Nostalgic."

"Kerise, look, I can see where this is headed. I'm glad you're helping someone out, but do you really think it's good for you to be around a small child? It's obviously stirring up a lot of memories."

"Yes it is. Things I've avoided thinking about for so long." She took a swig of water. "I never told you why I killed that man, do you remember?"

"Yeah you said you couldn't help yourself. I didn't believe you at the time, but I know you like your secrets. And you usually tell me eventually."

"Well here's that eventually. He mentioned her by name, Tarin. He said he'd found her, and that it hadn't been too hard to do so."

Tarin leaned back in his chair and exhaled through tight lips. "Now it makes sense."

"So I was thinking, if he could find her, maybe I could too."

"That's a big leap. He had access to files, records, people in the administration."

"And look at the contacts I have."

"I'm just worried that you're setting yourself up for more heartbreak. I don't think I could watch you go through that again."

"It's different this time."

"How is it different?"

"Because if I can't find her, I haven't lost anything. When they took her from me, they took away my entire world. They ripped my seven month old daughter from my arms. She won't have any memories of me. And the man I loved, her father, was taken away and executed. They told me he tried to run, but I know that's not true. Not even rapists get the death penalty. Rape an unmarried woman and you're locked away, but if you dare to fall in love with one you're not entitled to, that's the end of everything."

"I know, and look, see how raw it still is."

Kerise slammed her hand down onto the table, startling a pile of plates. "Yes it's raw. But that's never going to change."

"So why upset things?"

"And what? I just don't bother? I spend the rest of my life watching women walk around on The Hope wondering if that's her, or that's her, or that's her."

Tarin took hold of her hand. "You'd know her if you saw her."

"That's a nice romantic notion, but would I? I was barely given a chance to be a mother to her, maybe I could walk right past her, even speak to her, and never know. Do you know what kind of agony that is?"

Tarin shook his head and pulled his hand away. "I just can't bear to see you hurting."

"This is hurting. This is pain every single day. I let down Tale and Freda, and I'm not going to abandon Minnie. I can't. I need to do this. So will you help me?"

Tarin sighed and looked down at the table edge. "I suppose you'll just do it anyway whether I help or not."

"Exactly. And you know just about every dodgy officer there is. If there's someone we can buy, you'll know them. And I have a few favours I can call in."

"Of course you do. So where do we start?"

14

When Maeve came through the door into the refuge, the first thing she saw were the black rims under the sisters' eyes. It was like looking at a trio of pandas. And the reason the shadows were so dark, was because their usually flushed faces were so pale.

Maeve sat Faith at one of the tables, serving the girl with a plate of sandwiches and a drink while she quizzed the sisters.

"We haven't had any sleep at all," one of them said. "And neither has anyone else."

"She was wailing all night, thrashing about in her bed, like someone was attacking her."

"We moved everyone else upstairs and I swear she got louder."

"We couldn't wake her, couldn't get her to stop."

Maeve nodded thoughtfully. "Was she shouting anything in particular?"

"Most of it was incoherent, but there were a lot of violent words; about rape and death and blood."

"And a lot of profanities too. We have children here, they can't be listening to all that."

"Where is she now?" asked Maeve.

"She's finally sleeping. As soon as the sun was up, she slept peacefully."

"Well, let me look after the café today, and you three get some sleep. When Corinn gets up I'll talk to her, see if there's something we can do."

The sisters filed past Maeve muttering to one another.

"Maybe a tranquilliser."

"Or a sharp blow to the head."

"Or a bullet."

Maeve walked back to where Faith was sat. "We're going to be working here today. Are you going to help me serve people?"

Faith nodded, her smile full of bread. She had basically grown up here, and loved to help. Maeve let her lay the tables, or wash up plastic cups. She had even found her old pull-along cart and let Faith take things to and from the kitchen with it, despite the painful memories it induced. But it was nice, in a way, to finally let it be part of making new, happier ones. And the customers loved her, always commenting how happy and polite she was.

Even though the bell above the door still made Maeve cringe, she loved being here. It was comforting to see a house that, to her, was a scary dangerous place, transformed into a place of joy, hope, and sanctuary. Her father had left a wonderful legacy.

As she opened the front door to welcome

customers inside, Maeve pushed thoughts of her father from her mind. She needed to think about what to do with Corinn.

The café was busy through the morning; people used it as an unofficial meeting place, and the talk was all about the administration and the ID bracelets. Many of the women were wearing them, and they were walking back and forth to compare, or to show them to women yet to receive one.

One woman was showing off a nasty cut up her arm where her husband had tried to saw hers off. There was barely a scratch on the bracelet itself.

Others spoke of hearing it buzz in the quiet of night, or incessant itching underneath it. One claimed it had given her the power of telekinesis, while another claimed it caused her to keep forgetting words; although she had no problem telling her story. One thing was universal; the women didn't like the bracelets, hadn't asked for them, and intended to find a way to be rid of them.

By midday, the sisters were back again. They still looked tired, but it was a marked improvement from the ghosts they had been when Maeve had arrived.

"All quiet upstairs?" Maeve asked.

"For now. Looks like you've got things covered here."

"And I have my little helper." Maeve gestured to Faith who was stacking empty plates at a table.

"Well, Corinn's awake, if you wanted to go and see her."

"I suppose I'd better meet this girl who's causing so much havoc." Maeve rinsed her hands under the tap, and shook off the drops. "Keep an eye on Faith for me."

"Not a problem." One of the sisters trundled over to Faith and scooped her up, tickling her with thick fingers. Faith squirmed and giggled, but there was no chance she'd escape from that grip.

Happy that Faith would be well looked after, Maeve headed upstairs.

The landing was mostly quiet except for the odd footfall above, or a child's voice. But it seemed like the whole house was holding its breath, waiting for what might happen when Maeve met Corinn.

Maeve put her fingers on the door handle and pushed the door open. Corinn was sat on the bed by the window, looking out at the view. Maeve walked over and sat at the other end of the bed, but Corinn continued to gaze outside.

"Hi Corinn, I'm Maeve."

Corinn didn't respond.

Maeve shifted forward on the bed, closer to her. "Corinn?" Still nothing. She reached out and touched Corinn's hand.

The impact knocked Maeve backwards, and her head slammed against the metal foot of the bed. She didn't dare move as her vision trembled and began to grow dark.

15

As Kerise knocked on Marianne's office door, she realised her hand was shaking. Not because she was scared, nor because she was excited. It was simply because nothing had ever been so important to her.

She pushed the door open, too impatient to await an invitation, and found Marianne asleep on a small camp bed.

Kerise crouched and roughly shook the woman awake.

Marianne blinked and rubbed her eyes, her face furrowed with a look of confusion. Kerise shook her again.

"Stop, I'm awake, I'm awake. Blimey, Kerise, what the hell do you want?"

"You know I told you that if I found somewhere for Corinn to go, that you'd owe me a favour?"

"Yes. 'The biggest favour you've ever owed anyone in your life.' I remember."

"Well, I'm calling it in."

Marianne rubbed her eyes again. "Can't you

call it in when I'm more awake?"

Kerise ignored the request. "I need you to make some discreet enquiries amongst your customers who work for the administration. I need to find someone."

"Discreet enquiries?"

"Choose people you can blackmail. People who have a lot to lose."

"Who are you looking for?"

"A girl. She would be almost nineteen now. She was born illegitimately on The Hope and removed from the mother when she was seven months old. Her name is Minnie. As far as I know they kept her first name, but I don't know what her surname will have been changed to."

Marianne laid her hand on Kerise's wrist. "Is this your daughter?"

"I just need to find her."

"This is really dangerous. You know that, right?"

Kerise stood up, pulling her arm away from Marianne's touch. "Will you help me?"

Marianne was silent for a moment, and Kerise could read nothing from her face.

Finally she nodded, sharply, barely a movement at all. "I'll help you."

16

Maeve slowly lifted her head, inch by inch, with every inch introducing another layer of pain, dizziness, and nausea. Frowning, she brought Corinn into focus, and found that she had suffered a similar fate.

"What was that?" Corinn moaned.

"I have no idea, but it hurts." Maeve gripped her head. "Let's not do that again."

"What happened?"

"I don't know. It was like every single memory I have jumped into my head simultaneously. Every emotion too. Wow. That was like my whole life in a split second."

"Has that ever happened to you before?" Corinn asked.

Maeve shook her head, the pain returning along with instant regret. She looked down at Corinn's fingers laid on the bed.

"Do you think?" She nodded towards Corinn's hand. "Maybe if we're really careful. If we take it really slowly..."

"I'm not sure," Corinn replied.

Maeve could hear the doubt in her voice, the fear. It was in her own too.

"It's just...there were memories there that I'd forgotten. Images of my mum. Maybe I could find something to help me...I don't know."

"Corinn nodded carefully. "Maybe if we both lie down first."

Once they had settled themselves side by side, and padded the bed with extra pillows, they both closed their eyes and crept their hands closer.

Maeve felt her consciousness begin to waver, like a flag tugging at the edge of her vision. She screwed her eyes tightly closed and tried to focus on her hand creeping across the bedding. She could feel the heat of Corinn's hand, the slightest brush of her skin, and the memories raced at her again. Swallowing back the panic, she tried to focus, to organise the images, the emotions. They came with sounds, smells, even the sense of being touched.

She managed to hone in on singular memories, scrolling through them like microfiche records. Maeve scrolled back, as far as she could go. She found her birth, her first word, first step; memories that had faded far beyond her reach.

Pausing the flow of time, Maeve stopped on a memory of her and her mother singing together. She could smell her mother, hear her voice, feel her warm, strong arm wrapped around her. She could feel her mother's hair twisted around her fingers. She could hear her mother's heart beating, feel the rise and fall of her chest. She wanted to stay here forever.

But then the image began to fall away, fading and slipping. Maeve reached for it, but it was like trying to grab the wind. The bed beneath her became solid again, the sound of the slums, of Corinn breathing.

Maeve sat up, her eyes flowing with tears. "Where's it gone? What happened?"

Corinn held up her hands. "You mustn't be greedy." Her voice had changed from that of a frightened little girl to one of a strict schoolteacher.

"Give me my mother back," Maeve lunged at her, but Corinn dodged out of the way, laughing.

"You can't live in the past, Maeve."

Maeve sobbed into her hands. "Please, please, I miss her so much."

"It's just a memory, it's not real. Your mother's gone for good, stop looking for her."

Maeve looked up at Corinn. "How could you be so cruel?"

"I'm not being cruel. You are."

"What?"

"You're so desperate for the past that you've forgotten about the future. There's a little girl downstairs missing her mum right now, but instead of going to her, you're up here crying like a spoilt brat."

"What?"

"Look at yourself, you're so selfish. Faith is your responsibility, and she needs protection. All you want is the past." Corinn flicked back her hair.

"All you think about is yourself." She casually checked her nails. "I mean, do you even realise there's officers on their way down the street right now."

Maeve flew to the window, banging her head against the frame as she tried to look up the street. Corinn was right.

"I can make them go away," Corinn said.

Maeve spun round. "How?"

Corinn pointed to the window. "Just watch."

Maeve looked down at the group of officers. One by one, they slowed and stopped. They looked around as if they had suddenly forgotten where they were going. Gradually, they started to make their way back up the street, away from the refuge.

Maeve turned around and looked at Corinn. She was stood, as she had been before, casually, as if they were simply exchanging small talk.

"How did you do that?"

Corinn shrugged. "I dunno. I just can. I can protect you and Faith from anyone."

"And what about my mother?"

"You can relive all the memories you want."

Maeve tried to think for a moment, but she couldn't separate out the rush of emotions, and her logic was lost behind a wave of noise.

"Pack up your things, you'll come and live with us."

17

Marianne had been watching the door all night. She was tense, on edge, and, much to her annoyance, she had bitten off several of her manicured nails. But finally, the man she'd been looking for walked through the door.

Although Marianne didn't know exactly what his job was, she knew he did something with records and computers. She didn't think he was very high in rank, but he did have the one thing she really needed. He had a lot to lose.

Marianne hurried over, trying to look more casual than she felt.

"Gus, hello. We haven't seen you in a little while? How's the family? Adela? And your two lovely boys, Coy and Millard?" She crammed the names in; eager to demonstrate how much she knew about him. "They must be growing big. How old are they now?"

Gus cleared his throat. Marianne realised she had somewhat ambushed him the second he came through the door. She cursed herself for being so forward.

"Adela is well, thank you. And the boys, well, Coy's almost fifteen now, and Millard's just had his thirteenth birthday."

"Two teenage boys in the house. That must be fun."

Gus snorted. "Not sure that 'fun' is the word for it."

"I suppose you'll be looking for wives for Coy soon. With your father-in-law's position he must be high up on the eligible bachelor list." Marianne nudged Gus playfully.

"That man probably had a girl picked out for him the moment he was born. I doubt I'll get any say in it."

She laid a hand on Gus' arm and gently led him to a quiet table. "It must be hard, living in your father-in-law's shadow."

"I haven't seen the light of day since I married his daughter." He smiled grimly. "My parents told me not to try and marry above my class, but you can't help who you fall in love with, can you?"

"You can't."

"It's amazing that she managed to convince him to let her marry me. Everyone knew I wasn't worthy; a complete nobody."

"But you got the girl you loved."

"I did. And I love her as much now as I ever have. Every morning that I wake up next to her, I'm thankful for how lucky I am."

Marianne squeezed his arm. "That's not luck, Gus, you're a good looking man, and a charmer too."

He brushed her hand away. "I'm sure you say that to all of your customers."

She leaned in. "Only the ones I really like. Let me get us some drinks." Marianne clicked her finger in the air and a waitress appeared immediately. "Get us some drinks, and keep them flowing." She turned back to Gus. "So, where have you been? We've missed you."

"My father-in-law's been around a lot. He's been off work after badly hurting his knee, so I've had to play the dutiful son-in-law. Thankfully he's back home now. He enjoys my company even less than I do his. He just makes me feel so—"

"Inadequate?" Marianne offered.

"Exactly." The drinks arrived with perfect timing, and Gus took a big swig from his. "Inadequate. He's always judging, and looking down his nose at me. And he never tires of reminding me that he got me my job, even if it is a shitty one. He also loves to go on about how he produced a daughter, and all I've managed is two sons. It's hard to handle when it's a constant bombardment of undermining everything I do." He took another swig. "I mean, what makes him so much better than me anyway?"

"Besides the money, the position, his contacts..."

"I have contacts too. He doesn't realise, but from my first day on the job I've been brown-nosing and schmoozing all the right people. I have access to things my job doesn't give me clearance to access. Sometimes it pays to be the little guy. People's tongues get pretty loose when they think you don't have any power. I could show them." He emptied his glass.

Marianne caught the attention of their waitress and another drink was quickly forthcoming.

"Well I hope my girls don't make you feel inadequate."

"No, no, your girls are exactly what I need. They let me be in charge for once." He leaned in closer. "Don't get me wrong, I know Adela loves me, but there's always a thing between us. The knowledge that I'm only there because of her. Everything I have comes from her and her family. She'd never say it, and she probably doesn't even consciously think it. But I feel it. Even in the bedroom, I feel, I don't know, less confident somehow."

"Emasculated?"

"Yes, exactly, emasculated. But you ask your girls, I'm a bloody lion when I'm here." His drink sloshed out of the glass and over his hand. "A goddamn bloody lion."

"So I've heard."

What she had heard was the 'games' this man liked to play. But Marianne's girls were clever, and they didn't allow themselves into situations that left them powerless. They had ways of slipping themselves free from any of the supplied bonds, they had doors concealed behind curtains for a quick exit, or for backup if they needed it quickly. Gus didn't know it, but he was never alone with one of the girls. He liked to be in control, in every way he possibly could be. And he tipped very generously. If only his father-in-law knew what his money was paying for.

"So what are you looking for today, Gus? Can I organise anything a bit special for you?"

Gus' eyes flashed. "Yes, you can, I'd like that." He finished the rest of his drink and tipped the glass towards Marianne. "But I'll owe you one."

She patted his hand. "Yes you will, Gus. Yes you will."

18

Maeve groaned as someone tugged her arm. She pushed the sensation away and curled back into her mother's warm body. The tug came again, harder this time, and Maeve pushed it away more forcefully.

The third time it came, Maeve was vaguely aware of the sound of crying. She gripped hold of her mother's arm and screwed her eyes tightly shut. But her mother was already wavering, her voice fading as the crying grew louder.

"No!" Maeve cried as her mother's voice, her scent faded away altogether, and the sounds and stench of the slums replaced them.

She scrabbled at the air, desperate to regain the moment, but reality had finally pushed its way in.

Reluctantly opening her eyes, she blinked and looked around. She was sat in an armchair, wrapped into Corinn's arms. She was at home. Faith was stood next to her, her chubby hands placed on the chair's arm, her round face striped where tears had washed through the dirt. Maeve shifted and looked down at her. Her face was grubby, her hair was unbrushed, and her clothes were stained with urine. Tears ran down her pale face from raw and puffy eyes.

"Oh my god!" Maeve leapt from the chair. "How long have I been out for?"

Corinn shrugged. "I dunno, a day or two. I didn't have the heart to break the dream."

Maeve snatched Faith up into her arms. "A day or two? Who's been looking after Faith?"

Corinn shrugged with a slight smile.

"I'm sorry, I'm so sorry," Maeve whimpered into the toddler's tangled hair. "Mummy's back, and I'll never leave you again. Let's run you a nice warm bath. I'm so sorry, baby, I'm so sorry."

As she carried Faith into the adjoining bathroom she glanced back at Corinn. She had turned sideways in the chair, her knees hooked over one arm, her feet swinging back and forth. She glanced up at Maeve and lifted her eyebrows with a twitch of her head. The look in her eyes told Maeve everything: she was in control now, and she was enjoying every minute of it.

19

Gus had originally denied Marianne her crazy request. Because it was crazy. It not only put his job in jeopardy, but his life too. His life.

He looked down at the keys in his hand and then up at the impressive house in front of him. He hadn't earned this, and sometimes he wondered if he even deserved it. Of course, for as long as he could remember, he'd known that he was destined for bigger things, destined to rise above his humble roots growing up in a small terrace house on Lynstock. He'd always looked up the steps to Haverhead and known he'd end up there one day. But this wasn't how he'd imagined it happening.

The front door opened smoothly, and Gus knew he wouldn't hear a single creak from the stairs. He employed workmen regularly to ensure his sleeping wife never knew what time he came home at night. Or what time he snuck out.

He wandered through the dark house, his memory filling in the furnishings and objects he couldn't see. All things he hadn't earned. The only thing he'd done was to fall in love with the wrong girl. And he did love Adela, he loved her so much it sometimes drove him crazy, left him unable to sit down, unable to look at her for fear he might cry. And he loved his boys. He loved watching them develop into individuals, he loved watching them as they learnt something new; their elation at having achieved something by themselves. There was no joy like it. His heart ached with pride. There were days when he thought he might need a second heart to fit all of his emotions into.

"Do it for Adela," Marianne had urged him. "And do it for Coy and Millard. You wouldn't want to lose them, would you?"

In that moment, Gus had been left with no choice. If he tried to access restricted files, or if he happened to ask the wrong person to help, or if he was a little too loose with his tongue, it would all be over. He'd lose his job, his family, and most likely his life, but certainly his liberty. But if he didn't? Finding out about his trips to The Linden Tree would not be something Adela would forgive. Especially if, as he imagined she would, Marianne gave a blow by blow description of everything he'd done. His face flushed at the thought; he'd been as depraved as he could have been.

He tiptoed past the boys' bedrooms, pausing to listen to Coy's heavy breathing, and Millard's gentle snoring. He had let them down so badly. He hadn't been even half the role model he had wanted to be.

He nudged open the door to his own bedroom and looked over at Adela asleep in the bed. One arm was hooked around the top of her head, her hair swept out to the side, and she looked almost like a ballerina, mid-spin, her motion captured and caught like a butterfly's wings pinned down by a collector.

Gus had collected his family, but they weren't really his, and they could tear their wings free at any moment.

He sat on his side of the bed and stared out of the expansive bedroom window. The lawn below was lit by strings of tiny lights; it was magical, enchanting, like a mythical land. But it was just an illusion.

He could barely believe he was about to risk everything for a woman he had only spoken to a handful of times, but there was a chance, even if just a slim one, that he might actually pull this off. But if he'd refused, it was an absolute certainty that his wife would find out everything, and his father-in-law would make certain that he never saw any of his family again.

He clenched his fists. Marianne had him. And she'd only given him four days.

20

"How are things going with Corinn?" asked one of the sisters.

A flash of worry passed through Maeve's memory, and she instinctively reached out to touch Faith. But it was gone as soon as it came, and Maeve couldn't grab hold of it. Was she worried? She shook the unsettling feeling off. "Fine. No problems at all. She's actually been really good helping out with Faith."

"No nightmares? No screaming in the night?"

"Absolutely nothing." Maeve squeezed Faith's hand. "We like Corinn don't we?"

"Yes," Faith replied. "She tells me stories."

The sister sat down, the chair creaking under her weight. "What sort of stories does she tell you, sweetheart?"

"About the queen of the fairies."

"Well that sounds exciting. What does the queen of the fairies do?"

"She punishes the humans."

Maeve frowned. "How does she punish them?"

Faith shrugged. "Different ways."

"Like what?"

Faith dropped her hands into her lap. "I don't know," she muttered.

"That's ok," Maeve said. "It doesn't matter." She looked up at the sister, and that fleeting worry wormed its way back.

"Just keep a close eye," the sister said.

Maeve nodded and glanced back at Faith. "How are things going here?"

"It's tense. The whole of The Floor's tense, but you know that."

"It does seem like there are more and more officers here everyday. Corinn's managed to keep them away from our front door so far."

"There's been some flare ups with the locals, a few scuffles, and a couple of arrests, but nothing serious yet. But I can feel it in my gut, there's something big brewing."

"Well, you can't really miss the atmosphere of unrest."

The sister leaned forward, trapping her breasts against the edge of the table. "It's more than that."

"What do you know?"

The sister sucked her lips in and smiled. "They've been coming here to plan it. A big uprising. A riot."

Maeve laid a hand on Faith's shoulder. "A riot? When's this happening?"

The sister looked down at Faith. "Don't worry, I was going to give you the head's up. I'm sure that you can disappear up to The Hope for a few hours.

Get littl'un far away from it all. Two days. High noon. Just like in the good old days." She grinned.

"As if there's anyone alive to remember when any of our days were good," Maeve replied. "Thanks for the head's up. If only we had a real sanctuary to go to."

The sister nodded slowly. "We could all do with Father Harris right now. Has there been any news?"

"No. I check in occasionally with Brother Grant, actually it's Father Grant now, but if the abbot knows anything, he's keeping it to himself. Some days I assume Dad must be dead, because in three years they've not managed to get out of him where Faith is, and other days I hope he is, because the thought of them torturing him for years is too much to bear."

"It'll all turn right in the end. Somehow, it usually does."

The sister scraped her chair back and heaved herself back to standing.

"I wish I had your faith," Maeve said.

The sister smiled, and the corners of her lips disappeared into her cheeks. "When you're as old and fat as me, you'll realise that's all any of us ever have."

21

Gus smoothed out the screwed up note he'd just pulled from his shoe, and frowned at it. His sweat had smudged a couple of the letters, and he could barely read them. He rubbed his damp hands on his trousers and turned the paper over. The letters weren't any clearer from the reverse. If he got this password wrong it would set off alarms everywhere.

He took a deep breath and laid his hands over the keypad, as if it could somehow inspire him to the right answer.

"Here goes everything," he whispered, and slowly typed the password in, giving his best guess at the smudged letters.

He stared at the screen, willing it to accept him. He wiped the sweat from his forehead and glanced quickly around the room. No one was looking his way. That was the lucky thing about being a lowly minion; you were one of many, and completely invisible in the herd.

His screen pinged and he looked at it. He was

in.

Gus had committed Minnie's date of birth to memory; he didn't dare have that written down. He typed it into the search field, along with her first name and gender, and ran a search of the populace.

If he'd been searching for a male, he wouldn't have needed a password at all, everyone had access to those records. But searching for a female was a different level altogether.

Gus hadn't completely lied when he'd told Marianne that he had been schmoozing people since he'd got the job, he had merely exaggerated the importance of those people.

In The Compound, like stuck with like, and despite Gus' large house on Haverhead, and despite the status of his wife and father-in-law, people knew him for what he was. Like stuck with like, and he was no more than a lowly Lynstock boy. And no matter who he married, that was all he would ever be. No man could outrun his past. His father-in-law delighted in reminding him of that.

Despite the limitations of his status, Gus had been clever in which other lowly Lynstock boys he had befriended, and he had known that some day Claron would come in handy.

Claron was young, naive, and eager to please. He was also a genius when it came to computers. And the other thing about Claron, the very thing that Gus had used as a bargaining tool, was that he was a very horny young man.

The computer pinged again. No match found.

Gus frowned, but ran the search again without the name at all. Again, the search returned no matches.

Perhaps she'd been entered under a different date of birth to hide her. Gus searched again with her name, but no date of birth. Nothing. If all her details had been changed, he didn't stand a chance.

He drummed his fingers on the desk and glanced around, looking for a spark of inspiration. And then he saw her. There were very few women working for the administration, in fact, Falside boasted very few working women at all, but there were some. He watched her pass. He didn't know her name, or what her job was, but he suspected he'd be able to pick her bum out in a line up, he'd spent that long looking at it day after day.

He turned back to his screen and ran another search. This time, in the personnel database.

Convincing Claron to give up the password hadn't been too hard.

"I heard a rumour," Claron had said, "that you go somewhere where there's girls that you can...y'know."

"I do."

"Do you think you could take me?"

"It's a pretty exclusive place."

"I can tidy myself up, wear something nice. But they're not fussy, are they, these girls?"

"If you're paying enough, they'll do whatever you want. Believe me. But they're not cheap."

Claron shrugged. "What else have I got to

spend my money on?"

Gus leaned back, pretending to think it over. "I really don't know, Claron. This is a pretty exclusive place, and if you come as my guest, I'd be vouching for you. If you messed up, that would be my reputation gone too." He shook his head. "I really don't think I can do it."

"I won't let you down Gus. Come on. I've never...I've never...and I just want to. I really want to."

Gus pretended to think again. "Look, maybe if I had some guarantee that you wouldn't let me down. Some show of loyalty. Something to prove that you've got my back no matter what the risk."

"Anything, just name it."

The computer pinged and Gus looked back at it. He closed his eyes, and then looked again. It was true. Minnie was on the administration's payroll, and he knew exactly where she was.

22

Maeve woke to the sounds of yelling. She sat up, and automatically reached out to Faith who slept soundly beside her.

The floor was freezing, and a cold draught lazily slid over Maeve's bare feet as she swung them to the floor. There was a door or a window open somewhere in the house.

Stopping to pull the bed covers up to Faith's chin, Maeve pulled back the curtain that separated their bedroom from the living room.

She was right; the front door was wide open. She skipped across the stone tiles, the cold trying to bite at her toes, and closed the door, ensuring the bolt was pushed all the way across.

"They started early," Maeve muttered to herself.

Through a crack in the curtains, Maeve watched as Hole Street filled up with people. Many of them had armed themselves with makeshift weapons; crowbars, rakes, spades, even chair legs and broken pipes. Amongst the general noise of voices, a chant rose above as more people joined in:

"Leave the slums, you have been told
Our women and girls will not be sold
We'll stamp your bones into the mud
And run the river with your blood."

23

The sisters' faces were red and dripping by the time they had finished barricading the front of the café with furniture. They had dragged mattresses down from upstairs and tied them up against the window. They had pulled a dresser from the kitchen and pushed it in front of the door. Every table and chair in the café had been utilised.

The sisters crouched on the floor as one, gasping for breath and clasping their chests.

Upstairs, six women cowered on a single mattress, and three young children huddled together in the bath.

The sisters sat in silence, listening to the sounds outside. They jumped at every crash, every shatter of glass, every gunshot.

"You're not wanted here!" someone yelled.

"You have no authority!"

"We won't pimp our women to you!"

"We'd rather murder them ourselves than hand them over to the administration!"

The sisters looked at one another. "Do you

think they really would?" one sister whispered.
The other two dared not answer.

24

Corinn sat on the roof watching the crowds pass by below her. She leaned back and casually crossed her legs. It couldn't have worked more perfectly. She had only needed to place a thought in a few heads, and the madness spread easily enough. People were so easy to control, it was almost boring.

She heard Maeve close and lock the front door below her. She smiled, imagining her creeping back to bed, cuddling under the blankets with Faith, telling her stories or singing to her. Doing whatever she could to block out the reality outside.

The world was a cruel and violent place, and it was best to learn that young. There would be far less heartache that way. Corinn wished she'd had someone to show her the truth of things.

Still, this riot was missing something. It was barely the spectator sport she'd hoped for. Leaning forward, Corinn picked out a suitable subject below. He was big, clumsy, and singing the chant with gusto. He was also carrying a large, wooden stick.

At the end of Hole Street was a grocery store, its large front window too much of a temptation.

Corinn focussed on the man, and placing the thought was barely any work at all. He was a moron. She screeched as he swung his makeshift club into the window, sending cracks across it like spider webs.

Some people came to join him, with weapons of their own, while others tried to stop him. He shook them off and swung again and again, until the glass shattered around his feet. For a moment he stood still, confused, looking between the club in his hands and the broken window. But others surged forward into the shop, overturning baskets and shelves, and he didn't need any more convincing.

Corinn smiled broadly, shaking her fingers dry from the rainwater puddled on the roof. Now things were getting interesting.

25

Maeve gasped as the window broke and something heavy bounced across the floor. Faith began wailing, and pressed her body into Maeve's, her little fists gripping clothes and skin and hair.

"We have to move," Maeve whispered, throwing back the blanket they had cocooned themselves in.

"I'm scared, Mummy."

She gave Faith a squeeze. "I know you are, sweetheart, but I really need you to be brave, just for a little bit." She grabbed Faith's boots, and untangled the girl from her. "Come on, put your boots on."

"Where we going?"

"Somewhere safe. Come here." Maeve hefted Faith up onto her hip and pulled the blanket around them both. She knotted the loose ends around her shoulder, and tucked Faith's head inside.

Crouching, Maeve slid a tin out from under the bed, and tucked it into Faith's hands. "Keep this safe, sweetheart."

She crossed the living room in just a few paces, glass crunching under her shoes, and pulled the front door open.

The noise shoved its way in, threatening to knock her over. She braced herself against the door frame like a diver readying to jump, and then pushed off into the fast flowing crowd.

26

Corinn watched the young man heave back his arm and hurl the brick towards the house. She heard the window smash, and then she watched as Maeve and Faith pushed their way out into the middle of it all.

Corinn focused in on the crowd, but they were too divided; there were too many intentions to keep track of. There were people whose only thought was killing the officers, others who wanted to end things peacefully. There were those who simply wanted to cause anarchy, to loot, to destroy property, no matter who it belonged to. There were people trying to calm the situation down, and those who didn't even know why they were there.

The situation had gotten out of control, and Corinn could do nothing to pull it back.

Clambering down from the roof, she set off after Maeve and Faith.

Moving through the crowd was like swimming through rapids; Corinn was bashed this way and that, her body hitting against sharp elbows, hard, muscular bodies, bony knees. She bounced back and forth between them, until she barely knew which direction was which.

Rising onto her toes she searched the crowd for anything familiar.

"Maeve!" she screamed, but her voice was merely thrown into the mixing bowl with all the others.

Ducking her head back down, she pushed on, trying to bear the kicks and punches, trying to stay on her feet.

And then she felt a new intention reach her. Spinning around, she scanned the faces around her, trying to pinpoint where it was coming from. It was watching her, it was savage, and it was getting closer.

She turned her head this way and that, but the voices were overwhelming and this one kept slipping from her reach.

"Where are you?" she cried out, pushing her way backwards through the crowd.

She stumbled, and hands pushed her away. She turned around again, her vision blinded by the mosaic of faces, pressing in together, moulding into one mass of skin and eyes and teeth.

Fingers closed around her wrist and a voice spoke into her ear. "You shouldn't be all by yourself, love, it's dangerous out here for a pretty girl like you." The intention pressed up against her, sliding in under her clothes, searching for satisfaction.

Corinn pushed the man away, but he came back, stronger. She tried to turn around to see his face, but the crowd pushed them both forward, crushing them together.

The intention came back at her, impatient. Now was the time. Now, in this crowd. It snaked along her arm, anticipating the beautiful crack of her bones. It licked its lips, contemplating the sweet taste of her blood. It pushed in behind her eyes, and breathed in the scent of her skull. The skull it dreamed of shattering.

It was too strong to control, too intent to turn around. Corinn was the helpless young girl she had fought so hard not to be. She was the victim again.

The intention overwhelmed her, strangling her, spinning her eyes and dizzying her thoughts. She had no defence, no fight.

Thick arms closed around her, strong hands pulled at her arms, drawing them up behind her back. She involuntarily dropped to her knees. The mud beneath her was damp, cold, churned up by hundreds of feet. People knocked her as they passed, her head lolling back and forth, her eyes reeling as thick fingers traced down her neck. She closed her eyes as a knee forced her nose towards the ground.

"Please, please, please, please, please," she whispered into the mud. It was the desperate plea of a woman who had no one to pray to.

But someone heard, and someone answered. The hands left Corinn's body as the intent turned to panic before being silenced. The man dropped to

the ground beside her, his blood sloshing over her
skirt.

27

Kerise stepped into Marianne's office without greeting her. She stopped in the centre of the room and turned, slowly, to look at the man cowering on the chaise.

"Who's this?" she asked, gesturing with a slight cock of her head.

Marianne looked between Kerise and the man several times before answering. "This is Gus. My man from The Compound." Marianne stammered, ending her sentence with a dry gulp.

Kerise narrowed her eyes. "What's going on? Have you found Minnie?"

Marianne glanced at Gus again, just a flick of her eyes. "He has. But it's not exactly good news."

Kerise stumbled back, and gripped the edge of the open door behind her. "She's dead, isn't she?"

"Oh no," said Gus, finally looking up. "Minnie is very much alive."

"So what's the problem?" Kerise stepped forward and placed her hand on her hip, the action moving her coat back to reveal the large knife strapped there.

Gus rose to his unsteady feet. "I found her somewhere I didn't expect to. I found her on the administration payroll."

"She works for them?"

Gus nodded.

"But women aren't allowed to work."

"That's true, in principle, and within the general population, but there are a few women working for the administration. Not many, but a few. Women with specialist knowledge, or who show a certain aptitude for something. Sometimes the daughters or sisters of some of the directors. They're specially picked, and, well, they don't get to go home at the end of the day."

"They live there?"

"The Compound, The Watch, and The Eye all contain staff apartments. They're used by anyone who needs to be on site; some of the staff who work night shifts, and, of course, the women. The administration doesn't exactly want to broadcast their employment."

"And Minnie?"

"She works, and lives, in The Eye."

Kerise whistled. Maybe it would have been better if Minnie had been dead. The Eye was equally out of reach to her, yet she would now have to suffer the agony of knowing just how close her daughter was. Like trying to grab something with the tips of your fingers, only to have it move further away.

"What does she do there?"

"It appears that she has a talent for science. I'm not entirely certain what she does, it was a little confusing to be honest. Her job title is listed as 'Aqua-Bio Engineer'. Perhaps they're building some kind of marine-life army." He shrugged. "I don't know, I have no idea what it means."

Gus cleared his throat and glanced up at Marianne who nodded at him.

"I have something else for you," he said, pulling a folded sheet of paper from his pocket. He held it out to Kerise.

She looked at it suspiciously. "What is it?"

"Her staff photo."

Kerise snatched it from him, slipped it into her coat pocket, and walked out.

28

Maeve looked down at the hammer in her hand. She looked at the blood running down the handle, the hair stuck to it, the flesh. Blinking, she tossed it to the ground.

For a moment she couldn't remember what she was doing, or where she was. Noise and people crushed in around her and Faith's hot breath flared against her neck.

And there was so much blood.

"Are you ok my darling?" She began running her hands over Faith, still strapped to her hip, checking her for injuries.

"I'm ok, Mummy." She wrapped her arms around Faith's neck. "Is Corinn ok?"

Maeve frowned. She could taste blood on her lips. "Corinn?"

Faith pointed towards the floor, and Maeve followed with her eyes.

Corinn was sat in the mud, her dress soaked with dirty water and blood, her face white against it all.

Maeve looked down at the hammer, now being kicked about by stumbling feet. Then she looked back at Corinn who was now holding her hand out.

Maeve grabbed it and pulled her to her feet.

"Come on," said Corinn, already tugging Maeve through the crowd. "We need to get away from here."

"Wait," Maeve protested.

"There's no time," Corinn called back.

Maeve tightened her grip on Faith as they squeezed and careened their way through the crowd, led by Corinn. They made their way down towards the river, wading through deep, wet mud when they ran out of walkways to balance along. The mud sucked a shoe from Maeve's foot, but Corinn just pulled her onwards without pause.

They made their way to The Slip, which was eerily deserted. The brothel doors were shut, the lights off. There were no men loitering, no drunks, no cat calls, just the distant sound of The Floor rioting.

"We need to get inside," shouted Corinn.

"I know somewhere we can go," replied Maeve. "This way." Taking up the lead, Maeve weaved them towards Madam Lemaire's establishment. "They looked after me here before, I'm sure they'll be happy to do it again."

"Even if you are a killer on the run now?" Corinn called her reply lightly, but it hit Maeve like she'd thrown a brick. She was a killer, and they were all still covered in the blood that proved it.

29

Maeve stepped out of the still-steaming bath and allowed herself to be folded into the towel being held for her. Her skin was red and hot, and her wet hair clung to her neck. She was rubbed dry, and another towel was wrapped around her hair. She was powdered and given a clean nightdress to wear along with thick socks for her feet.

She was led to a bedroom and handed a mug of lemon water. Maeve wrapped her hands around it and let the steam dampen her face.

"Are you feeling better?" Madam Lemaire asked as she sent her girls away. "I hope they looked after you."

Maeve nodded. "They really did. Where's Faith?"

"Sleeping soundly after her bath. That was quite a mess you brought to my front door."

"I'm sorry. We didn't know where else to go. What about—"

"I've already sent people to deal with that. He'll be floating off downstream by now." Even talking about such things, Madam Lemaire was calm and untroubled. She stood straight, her hands meeting in front of her, her face giving nothing away. "So what's it like out there?"

"Awful. And certainly no place for a child."

"Neither is this."

"I suppose not." Maeve crossed to the bed and sat on the corner of it, her legs suddenly tired and aching.

"Still, you're welcome to weather the storm here. Until you can return home," Madam Lemaire added.

"If we still have a home to return to. They're looting and vandalising everywhere. Tearing the slums apart."

Maeve watched a flash of concern crease Madam Lemaire's face before she brushed it away. "Well, you're all safe here now."

Maeve smiled weakly. She knew that they were thinking the same thing. If the riot had turned into an excuse for random violence, then nowhere on The Floor was safe.

"I was sorry to hear about your uncle," Madam Lemaire said, her eyes looking anywhere but at Maeve.

"Thanks." No one had mentioned him to her in a long time, and it was odd to hear him spoken about with regret and sympathy. She hadn't even considered the fact that, despite everything, she had lost an uncle.

"He's missed around here." She looked down at the floor. "In a funny kind of way."

"I guess I miss him too," Maeve said thoughtfully. She caught Madam Lemaire's eye. "In a funny kind of way."

"He wasn't a good parent to you, was he?"

Maeve snorted.

Madam Lemaire sat herself next to Maeve. "There was some good in him though, and I want you to know that. He was very sweet when he wanted to be. He talked about you a lot."

"Really?"

"You didn't know?"

Maeve shook her head. "I thought he hated me."

"He felt guilty. About your mother."

"He talked to you about that?"

Madam Lemaire smiled. "Some men get very talkative when they're...satisfied and relaxed." She patted Maeve's knee. "You'll see."

"What did he say?"

"That you reminded him so much of her. You look like her, walk like her, talk like her. He was scared of you, I think, that you might be able to see right inside him like your mother could."

"Did you ever meet my mother?"

Madam Lemaire shook her head. "She was already gone by the time I met Lou."

"Did...did he ever tell you why he did it? Why he reported her?"

Madam Lemaire let out a long sigh. She chewed her lip and stared out across the room. "Yes. But I don't think that now is—"

"I want to know." Maeve cut her off. She

refused to be treated like a child, to be protected from the family secrets. "Tell me."

Madam Lemaire sighed again. "Your uncle was never a secure man. You know how he was; that ridiculous persona, the fake accent. That's what he was like, he always wanted to be somebody, anybody, other than who he was. He thought he was a disappointment to his parents. He'd never made much of himself, and everything he did have had come from his wife. He wasn't a doer, he never went out and worked for what he wanted. He schemed and lied his way through life. How could any parent be proud of that? But your mother was different."

"She was hated by everyone. Especially Papa. I only ever met him a few times, and he barely ever said a word to me."

"That's not how Lou saw it. He saw a remarkable woman that, yes, everyone feared, but a woman who was never afraid to be herself, no matter the consequences. A woman who stood up for herself, fought her corner, and held her head high, even when people were jeering and spitting at her in the street. Your mother had a strength of character and an integrity your uncle never possessed. And those were qualities he always envied."

"So he handed her over because he was jealous of her?"

Madam Lemaire nodded. "That's how I understand it, yes."

"Jealous?" Maeve repeated. "I lost my mother

because he was jealous?"

"I'm sorry that it wasn't what you wanted to hear."

Maeve shrugged. "It was the truth, and having that is a nice change I suppose. I guess I just wanted something a bit more worthwhile than sibling rivalry."

"I think most of the things people do come from very simple motivations. Love, hate, and everything inbetween. All any of us can ever do is act on our instincts."

Maeve stared at the steam spiralling from her mug. It all seemed so inconsequential. "It's like Mum meant nothing."

"He was threatened by her. He fought back the only way he knew how."

"At least he felt guilty."

"You see, he had a heart in him somewhere."

Maeve shrugged. "Of sorts."

30

Kerise unfolded the photo and smoothed it out. The colour had begun to flake where the folds had been opened and closed over and over again. She knew the placement of every hair on Minnie's head, every mole, every pore. When she closed her eyes, she found the image burned into the back of her eyelids.

Reluctantly, she slid it across the table, wincing as her brother grabbed it up with little care.

Tarin held it up to the light, as if checking for a watermark.

"So this is little Minnie, eh? This is my niece?"

Kerise nodded stiffly.

"And what did you say she did again?"

"She's an Aqua-Bio Engineer."

"What's that mean?"

Kerise shrugged. "Goodness knows. I guess they're working on things way more advanced than we could even imagine."

"So she's a smart cookie then." Tarin grinned. "She obviously gets that from her uncle."

"She's gorgeous and talented, she clearly gets nothing from you." Kerise reached out for the photo, but Tarin moved it further away. "Come on, give it back."

Tarin shook it gently and laughed. It was like they were kids again, back to the constant teasing. Kerise sat back and folded her arms. She wasn't going to let him rile her up like he used to.

"What's this?" Lucille appeared in the kitchen doorway and snatched the photo from Tarin's hand. Kerise jumped halfway from her seat, but stopped herself and sat back down. She didn't want Lucille to know how precious it was. Lucille would delight in destroying anything of importance to Kerise.

Instead, she leaned back as casually as she could. "Just a missing girl I'm looking for." She shot a warning look at Tarin.

Lucille grunted and tossed the paper back onto the table. "Well I hope you're not dragging your brother into another of your ridiculous plans. I need him here as a father, and a husband. That's what he is." She placed a fat hand of ownership on his shoulder. "How long before I can have my kitchen back?"

"Actually, Lucille, the health services are headed over to destroy it. After months of investigation, they've discovered that all of society's ills are originating from this very kitchen. They're going to evacuate the whole street."

Lucille's face began to darken. Her lips scrunched and wrinkled, her eyes sunk into her fleshy cheeks like setting suns.

"Fine." She grabbed the photo up from the table, stormed over to the worktops and began wiping them down with it.

Kerise flew from her seat, but before she managed to grip her hands around Lucille's throat, before she could reach for one of her knives, her brother's hulk stood between her and his wife.

He placed one hand on the back of the photo, putting a stop to Lucille's cleaning. He placed his other hand around her wrist, and moved her hand away from the soggy paper.

"You will have the kitchen back when we've finished with it. Until then, you will leave us in peace."

Lucille's mouth fell open, her bottom jaw rippling her neck into waves of surplus flab. Her eyes flitted between Tarin and Kerise.

"How dare you—" she started.

"Out!" Tarin wheeled her round towards the door. "Out, woman. Goddammit, just get the hell out of here!"

Lucille was propelled out of the kitchen, and Kerise stared up at Tarin as she heard Lucille collide with something out in the hall.

"You'll be in trouble tonight," Kerise said.

Tarin grabbed the worktop. "My God, I'm still shaking." He grinned at Kerise. "I wish I'd put my foot down with that woman years ago."

"I'm proud of you."

He picked up the sodden photograph and tried to smooth it out. The creases were so heavily folded in, that the paper simply tore open, Minnie's face gaping.

"I'm so sorry, Kerise." He pushed the pieces back together. "Perhaps when it's dry we can tape it up."

"Perhaps." Kerise looked down at the table, focussing on a dark stain in the shape of a rabbit. This room was full of stains, and she suddenly felt the need to be out of it. "I have to go." She stood up.

"Kerise, I'm sorry."

She didn't look back as she slipped out into the hall, and let herself out through the front door. She didn't look back as she hurried down the street, not taking care to keep to the shadows. And she didn't look back as she heard Tarin call after her, shouting her name out in a city that thought she was dead.

31

"How did you know?"

Maeve screwed her eyes shut.

"How did you know?" The question came again.

Maeve frowned as she tried to remember where she was, and what the answer might be. She opened her eyes slowly, blinking against the brightness of crisp, white sheets, and looked into the dark eyes of Corinn.

"What?"

"How did you know to come back for me?"

"Where's Faith?"

"Forget that. How did you know?"

Maeve wriggled her way up to sitting and untangled the sheets from their heads. She pushed the cotton away like she were unrolling clouds. Gradually, the world outside began to take shape. Maeve looked around the room.

"Where's Faith?" she repeated.

"Who cares?" Corinn snapped. "How did you

know?"

Maeve pushed Corinn away from her and swung her legs to the floor. She stood up and grabbed her head as the world began to spin. The floor beneath her tilted, and she fell back onto the bed.

Corinn's face appeared above her. "I wouldn't bother trying to stand for a little while, and walking would be impossible. Faith will have to do without you for now."

"What have you done to me?"

Corinn smiled. "Nothing much, vertigo's simple enough." She tapped her temple with her finger. "Especially when the mind is already weakened."

Maeve fought to get up again, but the dizziness brought a wave of nausea that filled her mouth with saliva. She gulped it down as Corinn gently lay her back on the bed.

"Don't worry, I'll look after you until you're feeling better. Everything will be just fine."

"I need to find Faith."

"I'm sure she's being well looked after. I need you to concentrate on me right now, or I'll make your legs useless for the rest of your life. It's amazing how easy it is to convince the brain of something that isn't even true. Even when it comes to physical matters."

Maeve lay her head back on the pillow and closed her eyes. Concentrating on her breathing, she tried to find Corinn inside her head.

"How did you know that I was in trouble?"

"I should have just let him kill you."

"How did you know?" Corinn repeated.

Maeve took a deep breath and exhaled slowly. She had found a knot inside her brain and began working to untie it.

"I really don't know, Corinn. The thought just popped into my head, and my feet just knew where to find you. I can't explain it any more than that."

The knot was beginning to loosen, but Maeve felt like she was untying it with frozen fingers.

"Try," Corinn said through gritted teeth. The knot pulled tight again.

"I don't know. Like I said, the thought just popped into my head."

"How? A word? A picture? A feeling?"

Maeve thought for a moment, her fingers fumbling over the knot, trying to find a loose thread, a flaw, a weakness.

"All three I think. I heard the words 'help her', I saw the man holding you, and I felt your panic."

"All three," Corinn whispered to herself. "And you're sure that it was 'help *her*', not 'help *me*'?"

Maeve thought for a moment for, pulling one part of the knot loose. "Yes. It was definitely 'help *her*'." She tossed one thread aside and began to tug at another. It was easier this time, and the knot began to open.

"Did you recognise the voice?"

Maeve twisted around and knelt up. The room around her wavered for a second, but then settled. "Stay out of my head." She wriggled to the edge of the bed and stood up, her legs sure of themselves this time. "I'm going to find Faith."

"How did you do that?"

When Maeve reached the bedroom door, she stopped and smiled at Corinn. She tapped her temple with her finger, and set off to find her daughter.

32

Kerise slammed the sheet of corrugated metal out of her way and ducked through the opening behind it. Fists wrapped in her hair, she spun around, trying to find some sort of solace, or relief, in the small, cramped space. But the half darkness offered her no hope, no solution.

She screamed, tucking her head into her chest, bending her knees, constricting. Part of her wanted to die in that moment, and the cold weight of a blade against her hip was too much temptation. She tore it free from its grip and hurled it across the room.

She would never let Lucille, of all people, have that kind of control over her.

Straightening, she focussed on simply breathing. She counted her breath in, and counted it back out. She flexed her fists and pushed the thought of her hands around Lucille's neck out of her head.

Folding her arms, Kerise closed her eyes for a moment. She was dizzy. Tired. She needed to sleep. Everything would be clearer then.

She swept a pile of clutter from the sinking sofa that wallowed against one wall, and lay down. She kicked off her boots and dragged a blanket over herself.

Something nuzzled at her elbow, and she lifted the blanket with a smile. A small, grubby cat crawled up to her chin and curled up, its fur brushing her face.

"You always know exactly when I need you, don't you?"

The cat purred in reply.

It was dark when Kerise woke, and that instantly calmed her. She reached out her hand, but the space beside her was empty. She stretched and sat up, shivering at the sudden chill as the blanket fell away.

"Abandoned me already, have you?" She looked around in the darkness, but couldn't see the small animal. "Still, you're not exactly my pet."

Standing, she crossed the room and flicked on the light. It buzzed above her, flickered twice, and gradually brightened.

This was one of several 'safe spots' Kerise had made for herself around the city, and perhaps her favourite of them. It stood on the roof of one of the taller apartment buildings on Lynstock, in a dead space between some service buildings. The walls around her hummed with the various generators and machines that surrounded her, but it had become a comforting sound, rather than an annoyance. It also gave her unrivalled views over the city and, more importantly, up to The Eye.

This was also the only place that contained anything more than the most basic provisions. Her other safe spots had medical kits, blankets, food provisions, hidden money and credits, hidden weapons, but this one was different. The walls here were covered with possessions. They weren't all hers, some of them belonged to complete strangers, but every single item was a precious part of her collection.

There were photos, keys, jewellery, odd shoes, lost gloves, books, pens, toothbrushes, hats, socks. Normal things. Signs that everyday lives carried on as normal, despite everything. Despite the administration. Despite the inevitable fate of every girl born here. Despite everything, people got up every morning, they got dressed, brushed their hair, breakfasted. They took photos of their family, they talked, laughed, went for walks together. They lived. Despite everything, they lived.

Climbing up onto the roof, Kerise crouched and looked up at The Eye. Lights set into the ground lit up the front of the building, lighting it like a candle at the very top of the city. A beacon. And that's what it had become to her. Something to look towards, something to hope for.

"I hope you're happy," she whispered into the night. "Somehow, Minnie, I hope you're happy. But I'm coming for you. Just you wait and see."

33

"How on earth are you planning on getting in?" Tarin asked. "They don't exactly take callers at the door."

"That's the clever bit. I don't need to get in." Kerise leaned back and folded her arms.

"So.....?"

"I only need to get them out. Maybe something like a fire alarm going off?"

"You're going to pull a schoolboy's prank?"

Kerise shrugged. "There's a reason it's a timeless classic. Because it works."

"And then what? When they're all lined up outside, what will you do then?"

Kerise nodded her head from side to side. "Ok, I haven't decided yet. Right now, I just need to see her. I'll figure the next bit out."

"This is the loosest, least thought out plan you've ever come up with, and I've known you do some dangerous improvisation before. But you're not on a reconnaissance mission here, or going up against some guy whose only crime is stealing pens from his office. This is serious stuff. This is gaining access to The Head, passing whatever security systems they might have, that you have no idea about, and slipping past the most highly trained officers the administration has, to what? Pull the fire alarm?"

"So I need to iron out a few creases. But I don't need to get inside. As long as I can get a fire going."

"Kerise, this plan is so thin, so pathetic, so ultimately hopeless. I can't believe you're even considering it."

"What would you do then?"

"Me? Honestly? I'm afraid I'd just give up. It's an impossible task."

"And if this was one of your boys? Come on, Tarin, you'd fight to the death to get them out of there. You'd go in with half a plan, or no plan at all. This is my daughter. My daughter who was taken from me."

Tarin sighed and leaned back in his chair, the wooden joints creaking under his bulk.

"Fine. But I'm coming with you."

Kerise flashed him a smile. "I was kind of hoping you'd say that."

34

Maeve peered in through the doorway. She reached out and gently pushed the door further open. It was only clinging on by a single hinge, and swung dangerously as she moved it. The inside of their house had fared little better.

"I'm so sorry," Madam Lemaire said, gently placing her hand on Maeve's shoulder. "Let's salvage what we can and head up to the refuge. See how well they survived."

"Hopefully they did fine. The women need a sanctuary in times like these." Maeve looked down at Faith. "See if you can find any of your toys, sweetheart. Just be careful, there's lots of broken things in there."

Maeve led Faith inside. "What happened, Mummy?"

"Just an accident, nothing to worry about. But we'll be staying at the refuge for a few days. That'll be fun, right?"

Faith looked unsure, but nodded, and set about looking for any unbroken toys.

The possessions they bagged up didn't amount to much; clothes and a blanket, a couple of toys, a book, two metal cups, and that was about it. Maeve set her jaw, refusing to cry in front of Faith. They were just things after all. They were both alive and safe, and that was what mattered.

"Looks like there'll be a lot of clearing up to be done," said Madam Lemaire as they picked their way through the streets.

Windows had been smashed, shops looted, personal possessions smashed and scattered. Some of the shacks had been demolished, and were now being picked apart by people looking to repair their own homes.

"It's so sad," said Maeve. "The people here have so little to begin with. Why would they do something like this?"

Madam Lemaire shrugged. "Who knows? Mob mentality? Blind rage focussed in the wrong direction? Maybe they were just so frustrated they felt better for just destroying stuff."

"I don't understand people sometimes."

"I'm not sure anyone does."

As they came out of Downstride onto The Wall, they found the same devastation. The main clashes between the administration and the slum residents had taken place here, and the buildings were pockmarked where bullets had hit.

"Oh my God," said Maeve. "This is so much worse than I thought."

They walked in silence towards the refuge, and as they reached it, Maeve clamped her hand over her mouth. The front steps were covered in blood, the front window was scattered across the ground, the front door had been almost split in two. She glanced around at Madam Lemaire, before hitching Faith onto her hip and hurrying up the stairs.

No one was in the café. The chairs and tables had been overturned, and the counter had been swept clean.

Maeve gingerly pushed open the door at the back of the café, her boots crunching over its broken glass, and peered down the corridor to the dark kitchen beyond. She listened, but the house was silent.

"Stay there," she whispered to Faith, passing the girl to Madam Lemaire.

Maeve crept down the hallway, her practised feet skipping the floorboards that creaked or cracked.

The door to the store cupboard flew open, the edge of it catching Maeve's elbow and throwing her against the opposite wall. A huge mass leapt out at her, brandishing something big and heavy above its head. Another hulk appeared from the kitchen, similarly armed. The hulks screamed, howled, and hooted like monsters from nightmares.

Maeve threw her arms over her head and screamed, holding her hands up in self defence.

"Please don't hurt me!" she cried out. "I'm sorry, I'm sorry!"

The two creatures silenced.

"Maeve?" came a familiar voice.

She dared to lower one arm and peeped out of

the crook of her elbow. Two of the sisters, red-faced and breathing hard, stood looking at her. They held large saucepans in their hands.

"Oh, Maeve," one of them said. "Sorry to give you a fright, we weren't expecting you."

"Who the hell were you expecting?" Maeve shrieked.

"Looters. We've already chased off a few."

A thick hand grabbed hold of Maeve's flailing arm and yanked her back to her feet.

"We could've killed you."

She rubbed her complaining elbow and looked back up the corridor. Faith was in Madam Lemaire's arms, quietly sobbing into her neck. Maeve sighed and returned to her, easing her away from her anchorage.

"Come to Mummy, it's alright. It was just the sisters playing a joke. Look."

Faith refused to lift her head from Maeve's chest.

"I'm so sorry," the sisters said in unison.

"Don't worry, she'll calm down. It's just been a stressful couple of days."

"I bet."

"Where's everyone else? Are they all ok?"

One of the sisters nodded towards the stairs. "They're barricaded in, and they're fine, if not a little frightened."

"What's it like out there?" the other sister asked.

"A mess, but calm. Mostly people trying to take stock and rebuild. Our house has been ransacked, but it's still standing, so we're luckier than some. But I was hoping we could stay here for a while."

"Not a problem. There's always space for one more. And we could do with an extra pair of hands."

Maeve glanced back into the café. "So I see. It's quite a mess."

The sisters looked at one another and grinned. "Most of that was us. We wanted to make people think we'd already been looted, so they wouldn't bother. Almost everything's safe in the kitchen."

Maeve smiled and shook her head. "Clever."

"But there's a lot of work to do, and before anything else, we need to make this place secure. We've got young children that need to know this place is safe for them."

"Absolutely right." Maeve pushed her sleeves up to her elbows. "Where would you like me to start?"

35

Gus dropped his head and slowly shook it. He pushed his hands under his thighs.

"No. No. It's impossible." He looked back up at Kerise. "There's absolutely no way. I don't have access to anything like that."

"You found your way into the personnel files," Kerise said. "Isn't that above your pay grade?"

"There's a big difference between personnel files and blueprints of The Eye. Can you imagine what they'd do to me if I got caught?"

"Can you imagine what your wife will do to you if she knows about your visits to this place? Or what your father-in-law will do?" Kerise glanced at Marianne for backup, but she was staring down at her desk. She looked back at Gus. "You've already hacked into files you're not allowed access to. It can't get any worse for you."

Gus shook his head again. "Of course it can get worse. Personnel files will probably lose me my job. My wife. My kids. My house." He counted them off on his fingers. "Blueprints? I'll be tried for treason, and God only knows what they do to terrorists."

Kerise folded her arms and leaned back. "Find a way. Or you lose everything."

Gus threw his hands in the air resignedly. "What choice do I have?"

Kerise stepped forward and patted him quickly on the shoulder. "Absolutely. Glad you're seeing things from my point of view."

He sighed and heaved himself to his feet. He looked at Marianne. "You really played me. I wish I'd never heard of the bloody Linden Tree."

Marianne kept her eyes focussed down.

Gus sighed again and let himself out of the room, closing the door quietly behind him.

"Don't you think you've gone a little bit too far?" asked Marianne, finally looking up.

Kerise shrugged.

"He's a decent man, deep down. He doesn't deserve this."

"Cheating on his wife with prostitutes? Yeah, he's a role model for all men, isn't he?"

"Not everything in life is quite so black and white."

Kerise huffed. "It is for the women of Falside, and he's the enemy."

"Because he's a man?"

"Because he works for them. Because he gets paid in blood money."

"Your daughter works for them too."

"Not by choice," Kerise snapped.

"You don't know that. She might be the most

loyal soldier they have. You don't know."

"Yes, I do. Let me know when he has something for me."

36

Maeve passed a fold of credits to the man and waved him off. She swung the new door back and forth, enjoying its smooth, quiet arc. She closed it and slid the bolts across. Then, she turned and surveyed the rest of the room grimly.

They had rescued very few of their possessions. The rest were either stolen, broken, or filthy. Maeve swiped a tear from her face. It was just a house. It was just stuff. Her and Faith were safe.

But it wasn't just that, and she couldn't pretend that it was. This was their sanctuary, the safe place they had built for themselves. It was where Faith had taken her first step, said her first word, called her 'Mummy'. This was their home. And it had been violated by her neighbours.

She picked up a broken mug, and pushed the two halves of it together. Faith's favourite. Painted with a simple pink flower. It was nothing much to look at, and had barely cost anything at all, but Faith had chosen it herself, and she'd been so proud as she carried it carefully home. Maeve winced as the sharp edge of it sliced into her skin, leaving a crescent of blood on her thumb. She rinsed it under the tap, the water icy cold.

Grabbing the broom she'd brought from the refuge, Maeve set about sweeping the remains of her home into a pile.

She didn't hear the bolts slide back, or the door smoothly open. She turned around as the cool air breathed on the back of her neck. But she didn't need to. She already knew who was there.

"Where's Faith?" Corinn asked.

"What do you want?" Maeve shifted the broom in her hands.

"Where's Faith?" Corinn repeated. "Where's Faith? Where's Faith?" She laughed. "You left without me, Maeve. That wasn't very nice, was it?"

Maeve shook her head. She could feel Corinn prodding and pushing. Trying to get in.

"You weren't very nice to me either."

Corinn rolled her head. "I wasn't nice?" She stepped towards Maeve. "I wasn't nice? I gave you your mother back. Has anyone else done that for you?"

"You didn't give me my mother back. You hypnotised me, and took me away from my daughter who needed me."

"We both know Faith isn't your daughter."

The old, familiar knot tightened deep in Maeve's stomach, and she fought to keep its presence from showing in her face. She tightened her grip on the broom.

"What do you want, Corinn?"

"I came home. That's all." She wandered over to the window and leaned casually against the sill.

"You're not welcome here."

"That's not really your choice."

Maeve lifted her hand to her forehead. The pressure was growing where Corinn was pushing, and pushing. Her thoughts were becoming fuzzy, sluggish, and she felt the broom slip from her other hand.

"Get out, Corinn." The words came out as little more than a whimper.

"Is that all you have? I thought you'd be more fun than this. The challenge I've always been looking for. But, no. You're just as weak minded as everyone else. Just as easy to control."

On her hands and knees, Maeve pushed back at the pressure, which had become a sharp pain. "Stay out," she grunted, sweat running down her neck. She screwed her eyes tightly shut and pushed hard, her back arching with the effort. But she did it. Corinn was gone from her head. Maeve looked up.

Corinn was gripping her own head in her hands. "How do you do that?" she demanded.

"Same way you do," Maeve panted.

"No one can do what I do."

Maeve struggled back to her feet and picked the broom back up. Its weight in her hands was comforting.

There was a flash of something in Corinn's eyes that Maeve had never seen before.

Uncertainty. Maybe even fear.

She pushed herself off the windowsill and stepped closer to Maeve.

"Who are you?" she asked.

"Who are you?" Maeve responded.

Corinn pressed her lips together and looked Maeve up and down.

"Why do you do it, Corinn?"

"Why not? Why not do it?" She sighed deeply. "People don't even want to make decisions. They wander through life waiting for things to happen to them, waiting for that 'one day' that they'll do this or that. They can't even decide what to have for lunch most days. They're weak willed, they're so weak willed that they're practically begging me to take over."

"So you're doing them a favour?"

"People need a push to do exciting things. They all live so safely. If you can call it living."

Maeve started brushing up the mess again. "There's a lot to be said for living safely."

"And die never having done anything exciting?"

"It depends on your definition of exciting."

Corinn was quiet for a moment. "I made something of those people. They'd have just faded away otherwise."

"That's not really for you to decide."

"Maybe."

"Corinn, can you just leave? I don't want you here anymore."

"I presume Faith is up at the refuge, right?"

Maeve didn't answer.

"It would be a shame if anything happened to her. Say if she wandered into the kitchen, found a knife, and just got the idea in her head to cut herself. Maybe cut her pretty little face up."

Maeve barely even knew what she was doing until the broom handle connected with the side of Corinn's head. The impact shook down the wooden pole, jumping it out of her hands. It clattered to the floor as Corinn dropped next to it.

Maeve looked down at her. She knelt and lay the back of her hand against Corinn's cheek. It was warm. She watched her chest rise and fall, and listened to her steady breathing.

"Who are you?" she whispered. Reaching out, Maeve took hold of Corinn's hand and closed her eyes.

The feelings reached her first; the fear, the pain, the sense of abandonment. And then his face. His hands. His belt. The sense of running, running until her feet bled, until her lungs burned. The bitterness. The desire for revenge, and the disappointment of not being able to satisfy it. But as Maeve picked deeper, she found the lies stitching it all together, and the guilt of betraying the one person who ever loved her.

37

Kerise dropped into the storeroom, and stood next to the open doorway listening carefully to the sounds of the corridor beyond.

Satisfied, she stepped out and walked slowly along it. Many of the doors were closed, with voices shut in behind them. Others stood open, awaiting their occupants for the evening. Their furniture was simple, adaptable, consisting mainly of tables and chairs that could be easily moved around to suit the intended use.

Walking into the main room, Kerise felt the immensity of it. It was a cavern, a void. She suddenly felt lost. Vulnerable. It wasn't a nice feeling.

"Kerise." Denver crossed the room in just a few strides of his long, skinny legs. "I almost didn't believe you when you said you'd be back."

"You left the window open though."

Denver shrugged. "Habit."

Kerise half smiled. "C'mon, you're glad to see me."

"Mixed feelings. It's always nice to catch up, but somehow, wherever you are, trouble's never far."

She held her hands up defensively. "No trouble."

"Just a favour?"

"I can't lie, there is something I need from you."

Denver crossed his arms. "I must be psychic." He sighed. "What do you need?"

"A uniform. A big one."

38

Maeve leaned forward and watched Corinn begin to stir. Her eyelids fluttered open, and her hand went automatically to her head. She groaned and slowly sat herself up, looking around with a frown.

Her eyes landed on Maeve. "You hit me," she said.

Maeve opened her mouth and managed to stop the apology tumbling out just in time. Instead, she said "I was nothing but a friend to you."

"I didn't ask you to be."

"I invited you into my home."

"Oh, please, you invited me here because you wanted to continue the lovely dream of being a little girl again. Of having your mother back. You used me just as much as I used you."

"That's not true."

"Yes, it is. You thought I had some kind of connection to your mother. But everything I created for you came out of *your* head."

Maeve nodded slowly. "You know what's really stupid?" she said. "I still want to help you. Despite everything, I still want to help you."

"That probably does make you stupid."

Maeve smiled tightly. "I know that you're not really like this. You're just lashing out." She thought for a moment. "Who did you betray?"

"What?"

Maeve watched panic pass across Corinn's face. "Who did you betray?" she asked again.

"How do you know?"

"Corinn I can help you. I want to help you."

"I don't want your help, I don't need it. You're not some magical saviour going round saving people from whatever personal turmoil you may imagine them to be in." She grinned, and the coldness returned to her eyes. Her mask. "Saving other people won't make your problems go away, you know."

"That's not what I'm doing."

"Really?"

"I just want to be a good person. There are too many bad people already."

Corinn grimaced comically. "You're sickening, saint Maeve. Not everyone can be saved. And not everyone wants to be."

"Oh for God's sake, Corinn, you're not the only wounded one. This place is shit, and it's shit for everyone. Everyone's lost someone, everyone's hurting, everyone wants to get out. You can't lash out just because you feel like it. It's not fair. Everyone's already got enough crap to deal with."

Corinn eased herself to her feet. "Well, I'm doing fine dealing with my crap by myself, thank you."

"Is that really how you want to live?"

"Come on, Maeve, that's how it is for psychics. Hated. Feared. You know that more than most."

"But you can have a safe place here."

Corinn shook her head. "Hiding. And with the administration very interested in the slums now, you're going to be hiding a lot more. They'll find Faith eventually. You know that."

"I can protect her."

Corinn threw her arms in the air. "You can't!" My God, you can't save everyone. They'll find her, they'll kill you, and she'll end up married to someone chosen for her who will bash her around and treat her like trash. That's her life. It's already mapped out for her."

"No, I can change things for her. I already have."

"A reprise."

"She's free."

"They've come for the slum girls, Maeve. No one's free anymore. You'll all be rounded up like cattle."

"Then so will you."

Corinn laughed. "If I wanted to, I could just walk out of this city, and no one would be able to stop me. I could walk straight up to The Eye if I wanted. I can remove all the officers from their posts." She cocked her head. "Maybe I just did. Maybe you could walk right out of Falside with Faith right now. Want to try?"

Maeve looked down at her hands. She rubbed

her thumb over the tattoo on her wrist. How long before she wore one of the administration's new ID bands? How long before Faith did?

"You have to help us," Maeve said. "We need you." A feeling of familiarity nudged into her mind. A sense of deja vu. As if she'd said that before. Or heard it. Or seen it written down.

Corinn placed her hand over her heart in mockery. "What? Join the cause? The fight for freedom? What even is that? When the women of this city were free they were raped and murdered. Besides, your resistance is long dead. You know that. The red haired girl ran away. The mousey girl gave up. And as for your warrior, she has far too much on her mind right now."

"Kerise?"

"Do you know what she traded me for?"

Maeve shook her head.

"The key to The Eye. And I'm going to help her open it."

39

Denver stared at the small packet of powder. He couldn't believe that he was about to do this. Grabbing three bottles of beer from under the bar, he poured them into glasses, and then looked back at the packet.

"You're an idiot, Denver," he muttered, as he tipped the powder into one of the drinks. He stirred it with a cocktail stirrer, a shiny pineapple adorning the handle, and left it to settle. "So much trouble. They'd have your head for this."

Loading the glasses onto a small tray, he watched the liquid glug from side to side as his hands shook. The corridor stretched out before him, seeming to grow longer with every step. He could hear the men; they were regulars, always booking the same room. It wasn't cards they played, it was some kind of game with counters that Denver didn't recognise. They shouted, laughed, threw punches, played big stakes, and drank. A lot. And one of them was huge. Denver only hoped the drug would work on this guy's metabolism. He was built like a buffalo.

Denver nudged the door open with his shoulder, and placed the tray on a side table. The men didn't even glance up. Whatever the game was, it was fast paced and required a keen gaze. Denver placed a glass by each man, carefully selecting the one with the added ingredient. He backed out of the room and closed the door quietly. And then he breathed out.

It was three hours later before the men emerged from the room. At least, two of them did. As they passed the bar, the older man lay a few credits on the counter.

"Seems our friend has had a little too much to drink tonight. We've laid him out. Alright if he stays the night?"

"No problem at all," Denver replied with a tight smile.

The huge man was lying on one of the small camp beds that were folded in the corner of the room. It wasn't unusual that one of his customers got too drunk to go home, or wanted somewhere to hide from his creditors for a night or two, or simply wanted to escape real life. The business relied on Denver being a man they could trust, and on The Paper Duchess being a safe haven.

The camp bed was bowed almost to the floor in the middle, and its springs groaned with every shaking breath the man took. Denver rolled up his sleeves, and looked at his skinny arms. How was he ever going to undress him?

Leaning over, Denver prodded his fleshy shoulder. He grunted, but didn't wake. Denver prodded him harder. He turned over, causing the springs of the camp bed to roll like ocean waves. The legs bowed outwards, but, somehow, continued to support the hulk above.

Denver looked around the small room, hoping for something that might help, but he found nothing. Still, Kerise said that, no matter what he did, the man would remember nothing, so if he could manage to wake him from his drunken coma, he could simply have him undress himself.

Denver grabbed the flesh of the man's upper arm and started shaking. The man grunted and snorted, and his hand tried to bat Denver away.

"Gerroff," he muttered.

Denver shook harder.

"Gerroff," he said again, and pushed Denver away. "Not tonight honey."

Denver grimaced. He couldn't believe what he was about to do. In fact, he wished he had more of that powder so that he could wipe this moment from his own memory.

Sliding a hand over the man's broad chest, he brought his mouth to his ear.

"Come on baby," Denver said. "Undress for me."

The man grunted and rolled towards him, his hands paddling, his eyes still closed.

"I'm so hot for you," Denver said. "You big, gorgeous thing."

A smile spread across the man's sleepy face.

"You bad girl." It was slow-going, it was clumsy, and it certainly wasn't a pretty sight, but when Denver finally left the room, he had an armload of officer's uniform.

40

Denver pushed the uniform across the kitchen table, toppling several pots and pans in the process. He glanced around. It didn't look like the kind of kitchen that required an apology.

"You might want to wash it first," he said.

Tarin pulled the jacket from the bundle and held it up against himself.

"Looks about right," said Kerise. "I'm sure you'll look very smart and handsome in it."

Tarin sneered.

"Good job, Denver. I was a bit worried you might not manage it, you know, physically."

Denver stood up and held up his hands. "You do not want to know what I had to do. I've had five showers and I still feel dirty."

Kerise laughed. "Well, you've done us a huge favour."

"And what do I do when the guy wakes up and wonders why he's in his underwear?"

"We'll have the uniform back to you tomorrow. Tell him he was sick and you sent it to be dry cleaned."

Denver frowned. He could only hope it would stall the man long enough.

"Placate him with drinks," Kerise offered.

"Great, so he drinks away all my profits while you guys are off playing fancy dress?"

"You're a good man, Denver." Kerise stepped forward and patted him on the shoulder.

Denver jumped away from her. "Don't touch me. Seriously. I need to go and have another shower."

41

Maeve tore open the tin, lifted out the journal, and placed it on the table. The sisters leaned in. It had become twice the volume it had been before, with the extra notes she'd slipped between the pages, trying to make sense of it.

She flicked through the worn leaves, trying to satisfy the thought itching in her head. She knew it was here somewhere.

She stopped, and smoothed out the page. "Here it is." She pointed at the words. "Look."

Caroline

Carolyn

Kaitlyn

Catherine

Cordelia

You need her. She ll reunite family. You need her. You need her. You need her.

"See?"

The sisters huffed as one.

"Remember that this journal was written by some crazy woman hearing voices."

"It hasn't even got the right name. You don't know that it means Corinn."

"She was hearing my mother's voice," insisted Maeve.

"Can you really know that?" Three hands patted her back. "Even if she was picking up your mum's thoughts, how many other voices might she have heard."

"Like a badly tuned radio."

"It could be that only half this book comes from your mother."

"Less even."

Maeve looked up at the sisters. "I have to believe that this is my mum, and that she meant for me to know this. I have to trust in that, because it's the only thing I have."

"You're a mother now, and you have Faith to think of."

"Corinn is poison."

"You need to stay away from her."

"Remember what she did?"

Maeve looked down at the page again. "Yeah, she reunited family."

"It was an illusion, it was dangerous, and it was cruel."

"It was malicious."

"Yes, you can't trust a girl who does something like that."

Maeve closed the journal. "But I can trust my mother. I have to."

She needed to mend bridges with Corinn. But first, she needed to find her.

42

Kerise frowned at the blueprints. All there seemed to be were problems, and Tarin, lounged back in his chair, barely even awake, was little help.

"You can stare at it all you want, we have no idea what we're walking into until we actually walk into it." He waved a hand at her dismissively. "Even adding in the scant amount of information I've managed to get out of people, it's suicide."

"There must be some sort of clue here. Look at all these lines running all over the building. It's got to be security. What do you think, laser beams? Tripwires?"

"Could be anything."

"Thanks for the help."

Tarin opened one eye and looked at her. "What do you want me to do? You're looking at a whole bunch of lines with directional arrows on it. For all we know it's an air filtration system because the boss has flatulence."

"Yeah, that's really helpful."

Tarin sighed and leaned forward. "Look,

there's no details on security here. We don't know which doors are guarded, or how. There could be finger print scans, retinal scans, hell, they might even want to check my DNA. We have no idea. None of the officers I know had even been up there. Everything we know is hearsay. And if we get this wrong, they're not just going to politely escort us off the premises, are they?"

"So what do you suggest? Just give up?"

Tarin pushed his chair back, the legs screaming across the kitchen floor. "Yes. Exactly that."

Kerise took a deep breath and laid her hands flat on the table. She stared at her bitten nails, and the congealed blood around the edges where she'd chewed too far. "Tarin," she said flatly, "your two boys are tucked up in their beds upstairs. Every night, you get to say goodnight to them, and every morning you get to see them again. You've watched them take their first steps, say their first words, go to school, grow into men. I had all of that, all of those chances, torn from my grasp. I had my entire future taken away. And here I am, with that future at the tips of my fingers, ready for me to take, and you expect me to simply give up."

Tarin stood and leaned on the table, taking one of Kerise's hands in his. "I'd never expect you to give up. I know you too well to ever expect that. But this—" he tapped the blueprints with his finger, "this is a crazy, impossible mission, even for you. Give up on this. Find another way."

"How many crazy, impossible things have you

known me do?"

Tarin half smiled. "I know, you do them all the time. You're something of an expert in the crazy and the impossible."

"And if there was anyone who could pull this off, it's me, right?"

Tarin stepped back. "I hate you."

Kerise grinned. "You love me."

"That's the trouble."

"So you're in?"

Tarin sighed deeply and gave a tiny nod. "But if you get me killed, I am going to be so pissed with you."

43

Kerise hauled herself up to the next fork in the tree, and braced her legs against the branch. It wasn't comfortable, but it was hidden, and gave her a fantastic view of The Eye.

Tarin was already halfway up the steps and, glancing around, he seemed to be alone.

He'd been right of course; they had no idea what they were walking into, and Kerise's efforts to find Gus, to get more information, had failed. Marianne hadn't seen him since their last meeting, and, despite several long surveillance sessions, no one had been in or out of his house either. Perhaps he'd gone into hiding, or perhaps...

She shook her head. She couldn't even think it. He might work for them, but he wasn't evil. He'd just made a mistake, answered an urge, and he couldn't have possibly known what would become of it the first time he'd walked into The Linden Tree. Of course, if he had been found out, Tarin could be walking straight into a trap. Kerise pulled a leaf from the tree and stripped it down to its skeleton.

She couldn't think about that either. This was a fool's mission, and Tarin was a fool for following her.

44

Tarin lifted his foot onto the top step and looked up at the stone lion looming over him. This was it. There was no going back now. His boots felt like they were filled with rocks, his knees like they were made of rubber. This was it.

He heaved himself up onto the level, and looked around. Fighting the urge to turn and look for Kerise in the trees, he pushed his hands into his pockets and walked up the path as normally as he could manage. He imagined he was walking like a newborn giraffe; stiff, shaky legs going in all directions. He was bound to call attention to himself. But the level, at least for now, appeared to be deserted.

The façade of The Eye was lit in a soft yellow glow, the pillars throwing dark shadows onto the windows behind. This place was awe inspiring in the daylight, but at night it was truly terrifying. The administration knew something about inducing fear.

Halfway up the path, Tarin veered onto the grass, aiming to find his way around the side of the building. The blueprints had shown a service entrance, which they had assumed would be less guarded, have less security features, than any of the main entrances. Although this place didn't appear to be guarded at all. That was what worried Tarin. If he'd been met with an onslaught of bullets it would have been better than the hollow feeling deep in his stomach right now. Something felt really wrong.

He tugged at the tight jacket and ducked his head down. Maybe it was a shift change. Kerise said she'd studied the security routines here, as best she could from the trees on Newstone at least, and he had to trust that she knew what she was doing. That was all he had right now.

As he approached the end of the building, he heard voices, and froze, one boot hovering above the grass. The voices stopped, followed by "ssshhhh". Whoever it was, had already seen him.

He proceeded slowly, almost completely deafened by the blood rushing through his ears.

"Evening," said a voice.

Tarin squinted. There were three figures leaning against the wall. Beside them, the service entrance stood ajar, propped open by a rock.

"Just having a quick smoke," another voice said. As if to prove its point, an orange glow flared as it sucked on a cigarette. The sweet scent of marijuana was unmistakable.

"I've seen nothing," replied Tarin, holding up his hands.

An arm was extended, the hand offering up a

hand-rolled cigarette. Tarin took it, and placed the damp paper between his lips, breathing in deeply.

The men laughed. "You're an accomplice now. Couldn't report it if you wanted to."

"Precisely," Tarin replied, exhaling smoke into the cool night air. Handing the cigarette back, he gestured to the service door. "I'll just sneak back in this way."

One of the guys held the door open for him. "Have a good evening, and remember to step over the alarm." He pointed down towards the floor.

Tarin looked; a thin black line ran across the honey-coloured tiles. He nodded. "Of course," and stepped over it and into The Eye.

The corridor itself was empty and featureless. The white walls stretched ahead like a pipe, boasting no doors or windows. This was not what the blueprints had shown, there should be numerous doors on both sides. They hadn't even considered the possibility of the plans being out of date. Tarin cursed his sister, and not for the first time that night.

He glanced back at the door he'd just come through. It wasn't too late. He could just walk away.

A mechanical system clicked somewhere ahead, and metal slid against metal. A man, dressed in a white coat, stepped into the corridor. Tarin bowed his head and turned away. Another click and slide. Tarin looked up. The corridor was empty again. So there were doors.

Walking slowly, Tarin ran his hand along the tiled wall. He felt the tiniest lip where a section stood slightly recessed. A small hole, the size of a fingertip, sat at the corner of one tile.

Tarin pulled off one of his gloves, and gently pressed his finger into the hole. Inside, a catch shifted, the door clicked, and slid to one side.

Inside, the room was lit only with emergency lighting; a sickly green glow puddled on a concrete floor. Pipes criss-crossed the room like brambles. They varied in gauge, in material, and while some were rusted, or green with algae, others looked as if they'd been installed yesterday. All of the pipes hummed as they gently vibrated, and the room sounded like a hive of bees.

The door slid back into place, and Tarin blinked. He turned, deep in thought, and the weight of a bottle in his pocket hit against his hand. He needed to stay focussed, no matter what he saw.

He walked slowly, looking carefully for the doors, counting them as he went. He stopped again, and looked down at the small hole on the fifth door.

A cool draft flew up the corridor, hitting Tarin's cheek. The door at the far end had swung open, and the men who had been smoking outside swaggered in. Their noisy chatter sullied the sterility of the corridor, and Tarin found himself cringing.

They approached him, and Tarin did his best to look casual.

"What detail are you on?" one of them asked. "There's no officers on this corridor after hours."

Tarin shrugged. "Just taking a short cut."

Another man slapped the first playfully on the

arm. "Perhaps he's just looking for a sneaky peek. Wouldn't blame him. Few men are lucky to see such a sight these days."

"Can't see much though," the third man added. "It's barely worth the effort of sneaking about."

Tarin grinned. "Yeah, you got me. You guys couldn't…"

The men laughed and nodded amongst themselves.

"Why not, eh? But it'll have to just be through the obs room, the holding rooms are monitored overnight, and what with the recent trouble, most of the officers are busy down there. It does mean security up here is pretty lapse." He gestured to Tarin's uniform. "As you well know. C'mon." He nodded up the corridor and Tarin followed him.

The observation room was located around the corner, in a corridor identical to the first. In his head, Tarin turned the image of the blueprint to keep his bearings.

As the man placed his finger into the hole, he lay his other hand flat against the tile above it. The tile glowed, and after a moment, the door clicked and slid back. The room inside was cramped, and loaded with maintenance tools. A grubby window sat high in one wall, with a tatty step stool placed below it. This was clearly an unofficial observation room.

"Enjoy," the man said, gesturing to the window. "When you're done, you can just open the door, there's no palm reader on this side." He nudged Tarin's elbow. "And clean up after yourself." He laughed, and let himself out of the room.

Tarin stepped up to the stool. It didn't look anywhere close to being strong enough to bear his weight, but the window was low enough for him to see through if he stood on tip toes.

He looked down into a large room below. At first, all he could see was pipework. It was more of a tangle than he'd seen in the other room, and the pipes here shook wildly and crashed against one another. Several people in white coats darted around them, pointing out and noting down anywhere water dripped from loose connections, and a mass of officers followed them, trying to hold the pipes still. Tarin looked harder. What exactly was the sight he was supposed to be enjoying.

Then he spotted one. A woman, naked, sat in the centre of a knot of pipes. She had her eyes closed, and she swayed back and forth, her head lolling, as the pipes pulled her one way and then the other. The man had been right; there wasn't much to be seen. The pipes came so close to her body, in such concentration, that barely any of her was visible. Tarin looked around the room and counted eight more.

In the centre, raised up on a plinth, another woman was in the pipes. But she wasn't being pulled around by them, she was the one causing them to move. She thrashed and fought, as if trying to get free. Several officers had hold of her, but she appeared to be stronger than all of them, and frequently wrenched her arms and legs from their grip.

The woman's head snapped around and her open eyes flew up to look at Tarin. Her mouth opened and closed as she screamed out words, but the window blocked out all sound. She pulled an arm free again and reached out to him. Tarin ducked down, his heart pounding.

He waited a minute or two before slowly peering back through the window. The woman was still, lying back against two officers, her eyes now closed and her mouth slack. A woman in a white coat stepped back from her, an electronic syringe in her hand. Tarin recognised her from the photo. It was Minnie.

He stepped back from the window and tapped his pockets. One bottle in each. It was time to get to business, he wasn't going to learn anything staring at naked women.

The corridor outside was empty again, and Tarin made his way back to the first hallway. Three doors down. The door slid open at Tarin's touch and, with a glance around him, he stepped inside.

The room was small, and packed with cleaning and equipment. A line of generators hummed along one wall, and one of the wall lights flickered and clicked.

Tarin looked up at the ceiling. The square duct of the air filtration system sat in a channel in the concrete, breathing gently. As Tarin stepped under it, it ruffled his hair, and whispered to him. 'Go on, I dare you,' it said. But Tarin had never turned away from a dare in his life.

He reached up and flicked the grille open. It

swung down like a dislocated jaw, and the duct sighed. Then he drew the bottles from his pockets. In the first, the raw, sterile scent of bleach, in the second, the acidic snap of vinegar. He didn't wait to see what they smelt like after he'd mixed them together.

Tarin watched everyone staggering from the building. They came out coughing, their eyes streaming, their arms folded across their faces. He scanned for Minnie's face. She was one of the last to exit, barely able to stand upright for coughing.

He leapt forward and grabbed hold of her, helping her across the gravelled path, sitting her down on the cold, damp grass. He pulled a water bottle from his jacket pocket and poured it over her face, rinsing out her eyes.

"Thank you, thank you," she gasped between bouts of coughing.

"Make sure you see the medics," Tarin said to her, before pushing Kerise's letter into her pocket. "I have to go now."

Minnie nodded and coughed again. By the time she finally caught her breath, Tarin was back on Newstone.

45

Through swollen, streaming, stinging eyes, Minnie watched the officer walk away. He wasn't like the rest of them; so bloated by their own sense of self, somehow believing that their uniform gave them a right to do as they pleased. It was damn hard to be a woman in Falside, but it was near impossible being one in The Eye.

Another cough convulsed through her body, and she spat the foul-tasting phlegm onto the lawn.

They would flush through the air filtration system soon enough, but Minnie wouldn't get back down to the Main until at least tomorrow. It was likely that no one would. At least she'd thought to stay behind and mask the women before she left.

The medics had finally arrived, fussing around everyone, but not really doing very much at all.

A young medic approached her, his hair and skin still slick with pubescent greasiness. He thrust a bottle of water at her awkwardly, looking anywhere other than at her.

"You need to wash your eyes out." He

gestured towards the building. "It was chlorine gas apparently."

"I know," snapped Minnie. She snatched the bottle from his hand. "I can smell it. Bloody hell, I can taste it. I'm not stupid."

The medic cleared his throat. "Err...I can bring you an oxygen mask if you'd like."

"I'm fine." Minnie struggled to her feet, ignoring the stick-like hand he offered. A cough fought its way up out of her and bent her double.

"I'll...erm..." The medic scuttled away and returned with a mask for her.

She took it from him and slipped it over her head, nodding her thanks, and offering him a half smile. She'd been unnecessarily rude. But it was hard not to be defensive when most men she met groped with either their eyes or their hands, and the rest of them couldn't even look in her direction. All she wanted was to be treated like a human.

The oxygen was a welcome relief, however, and eased the burning in her throat and chest. It also made her a little light headed, so she reluctantly sat back down.

She slipped her hands into her pockets, and closed her fingers around the envelope the officer had put there. Whatever it was, it would have to wait until she was in the privacy of her room.

By the time the medics cleared Minnie to leave, the sky was beginning to lighten. With her eyes sore from tiredness as well as the chlorine, she stumbled towards the staff quarters behind The

Eye.

"That was pretty crazy, huh?"

Minnie blinked and squinted up at Hector; one of the newest recruits to the Main, and one of the very few men who spoke to her as an equal, despite being her junior by several pay grades. But, she liked him. He was eager and ambitious, and he'd worked his way up to The Eye on his own merit, not his family name. In fact, as she understood, his family were nobodies as far as the administration were concerned. It was refreshing.

Minnie nodded. "Yeah, it really was."

"Do you think the women will be alright?"

Minnie smiled. The other engineers spoke about them as commodities, as objects, but Hector, like her, actually saw them as people.

"I masked them before I left."

"That was an unnecessary risk."

"It was entirely necessary."

Hector touched her arm. "You're right. I'm sorry, I should have stayed to help."

"Don't worry about it. I wouldn't want to be responsible for you as well."

"When do you suppose they'll let us back in?"

"It'll be hours yet I suppose. I'm going to go and get some sleep. Try to shift the pounding in my head."

"Will the Mother be alright?"

"She was doped up just before it happened, but you know how strong she is. I gave her enough to knock out an ox, but she's probably roused already. Goodness knows what damage she might do before we can get back down there."

Hector shrugged. "Well, nothing we can do about it now. I guess sleep is the best option."

"My bed is calling." She nodded towards the far end of the building, where the small handful of women lived, segregated from their male co-workers.

"Of course. I'll see you later." He winked and strode off on his gangly legs.

Unable to shift the smile from her face, Minnie wandered towards her room.

Once her door was closed and locked, Minnie scuttled to the bed. She kicked off her shoes and pushed the pillows into the corner to lean against. Sitting cross-legged, she slipped the envelope from her pocket and looked at it. It was completely plain. No name written on the front, no return address, no logos, no watermarks. It wasn't administration stationery.

Minnie frowned and tore along the top flap with her thumb. She read the folded note inside with wide eyes. And then she slipped out the second fold of paper. She carefully opened it and looked at the hairs enclosed. Their roots still attached.

The day had finally come.

46

Maeve stared across the small market. She'd spent almost a week looking for Corinn, and there she was, selling fish. She laughed at a customer's joke and met Maeve's eye.

Maeve nodded to her and made her way slowly through the silt.

The fish market was held right on the edge of the Falwere River, as deep into the saturated mud as it could be. As quickly as the fish was being sold, more was being brought out of the water, still thrashing and gasping. You couldn't buy fresher produce.

Corinn was scooping crayfish from large boxes and measuring them into smaller pots. She laughed and joked with the man working next to her, and he placed a muscular arm around her shoulders and squeezed her tight.

"Hello Maeve," Corinn said brightly.

"A friend of yours?" the man asked.

"Is it alright if I catch up for a bit? I think Maeve might have something important to ask me." Corinn flashed her a smile, but her eyes were full of malice.

"Sure sweetheart, but don't be too long."

Corinn pulled off her apron and led Maeve away from the market.

"Who's he?" asked Maeve.

"My father." Corinn giggled. "Well, he thinks he is. Ask him and his wife, and they can tell you all about my childhood. Even the day I was born. The memories are real to them."

"That's horrible."

"Is it? They've never been able to have children despite years of trying. Now they have one that they love. They're happy, and I have a good home with kind parents. Everyone wins."

"But it's still deceitful."

Corinn smiled coldly. "And if I asked Faith who her mummy is?"

Maeve opened her mouth to protest, but there was no argument. She was doing the same thing.

"But anyway, you didn't spend a week looking for me to discuss parenting, did you?"

Maeve looked down at the ground. "I think I might need you," she said tightly.

"Oh really? Your powers not good enough that you come running back to me. Maybe I'm not quite so evil after all."

Maeve sighed deeply, and pushed her hands into her pockets. They ached to be around Corinn's neck, and she couldn't trust them.

"My mother was sending out messages, prophecies, and there was someone listening. They wrote them all down. Most of it makes no sense, but there's something in there about you. At least, I think it's about you. My mother thought that you were important."

"What am I supposed to do that's so important?"

"Reunite family."

Corinn grinned widely. "Didn't I do that already? I don't remember you being too grateful though."

"I don't think my mother meant wrapping me up in some kind of fantasy dream world while Faith fends for herself."

"Look, if you want to go and play Joan of Arc dress-up, that's up to you, but I have very little interest in your revolution. So you go back to being a make-believe mummy, and I'll go back to being a make-believe daughter."

"I hoped we could put everything behind us."

"No, you hoped I'd jump at the chance of becoming a good person with a deeper purpose. Sometimes having fun is all we have, I don't know why everyone snubs the idea so much."

"Because we have responsibilities."

"If your mother was right about her prophecy then, somehow, I'll end up as part of this anyway. If not, well, I was never needed in the first place."

Maeve looked at her. It wasn't even the callousness that made her hate Corinn. It was the indifference.

"Fine. I'm sure we can manage without you."

"I'm sure you can."

47

Kerise dropped down from the branches. "Minnie," she whispered.

Minnie spun round, her hand laid over her heart.

Kerise stepped out from the deep shadow of the tree and looked at her daughter. She soaked up the vision of her; every tiny detail, marking it down, locking it into her mind. She breathed in deeply as if she could breathe part of Minnie into her. She clenched her fists, fighting the urge to grab hold of her. She knew that she'd never be able to let go.

Minnie stood awkwardly, her eyes flitting around.

"I know this is weird," Kerise offered.

Minnie nodded and cleared her throat.

"I guess you ran the test. You wouldn't be here otherwise."

She half smiled. "Yep, you're my mum."

Kerise nodded. "I never wanted to give you up, by the way. I don't know what they told you."

"They never told me anything. I was a ward of

the state. Raised, and owned, by the administration. Whenever I asked questions, they were answered with nothing but hard stares, so I stopped asking."

"You were wanted. You were so, so wanted. I need you to know that."

Minnie nodded. "I always wondered. Where's my father?"

"Dead. I presume. The administration took him before you were born. They came back for you when you were seven months old."

"Why?"

"You were illegitimate. I just fell in love with someone I wasn't allowed to."

"Why come and find me now?"

Kerise shrugged. "I should have come sooner, I know that, but this isn't easy."

"I know." Minnie glanced over her shoulder. "I don't have long."

"What's happening in there?"

"Far too much to explain." She glanced behind her again. "I presume I can trust you?"

Kerise reached out to touch Minnie, but stopped her fingers short. "Of course." She smiled. "I'm a revolutionist."

"The administration is losing control. They're not the ones doing all this, not anymore. The psychics, they're rebelling."

"What do you mean?"

"The population were unknowingly fed chemicals to reduce the chances of girls being born, but the psychics are stopping it now. There aren't nearly enough women anymore. This isn't control anymore, this is a catastrophe." She looked back towards The Eye. "There's so much more to tell you, but I can't stay any longer." She took a couple of steps back.

"Please don't go. Not yet."

"We'll meet again, I promise. I have so much more to tell you, and I think you might just be the exact person to tell. Something has to break soon, and it's either going to be the administration, or the population. No matter what happens, this is all coming to an end." She took another step back.

"I'll help however I can."

"I'll be in touch." Minnie turned to go, but then she raced into Kerise and threw her arms around her neck. "I knew you'd come for me."

Kerise buried her face into Minnie's hair and kissed her. "I won't let you go again," she said.

And then Minnie was gone, running back across the lawn, and Kerise was left with nothing but the fading warmth of her.

Epilogue

Corinn wrapped the stray piece of cotton around her finger, pulling it tight enough to turn her fingertip red. She leaned back and looked up at the ceiling. She could hear her new parents arguing upstairs. This new life was beginning to get boring. Plus, she hated the smell of fish. Maybe it was time for a change.

She stood up and wandered out into the cool evening air. It had rained for most of the afternoon, and she quickly found her bare feet sucked into the silt with every step. She pulled her skirt into her fist, and fought her way down to the river.

The water was freezing, and its first touch made her gasp. Despite the cold chewing deep into her legs, she waded further out, until the water was almost waist deep. Plunging her hands into the gently flowing river, she closed her eyes and let her mind reach out.

It wandered through the streets of The Floor, slipping under doors, creeping in through open windows, probing, questioning, listening in. It went further, to The Wall, up the steps, onto The Hope. It found its way, in the growing darkness, to The Compound. It slipped past the security, and descended to the underground levels. And there, it found Thad Quinn.

Thad was almost asleep, slouched in an uncomfortable chair. Bored. His mind was empty and waiting for the thought that Corinn placed there.

Grabbing his hat, he stood up, shook himself awake, and set off down the short corridor. At the third door he stopped, pulled the keys from his pocket, and unlocked the door. He walked in and looked at the man lying on the bed.

He was thin, unshaven, his eyes hollow and his mouth a grim line. But even reduced to this, he had something about him. A sureness. A resolve. A purpose.

"Get up," Thad said, the words jumping from his mouth without him even thinking.

The prisoner propped himself up on his elbows, although his arms looked thin enough to snap.

"Get up," Thad repeated.

Slowly, shakily, the prisoner complied.

"It's your lucky day. You're being released."

The prisoner frowned and stepped back. "What? Are you sure?"

Thad thought for a moment. "Yes," he replied hesitantly. "Yes, Father Harris, you're being released."

ABOUT ANGELINE TREVENA

Angeline Trevena was born and bred in a rural corner of Devon, but now lives among the breweries and canals of central England with her husband, their two sons, and a rather neurotic cat. She is a horror and fantasy writer, poet, and journalist.

In 2003 she graduated from Edge Hill University, Lancashire, with a BA Hons Degree in Drama and Writing. During this time she decided that her future lay in writing words rather than performing them.

Some years ago she worked at an antique auction house and religiously checked every wardrobe that came in to see if Narnia was in the back of it. She's still not given up looking for it.

Find out more at www.angelinetrevena.co.uk

ACKNOWLEDGEMENTS

It turns out that my mum reads the acknowledgements page before reading the book, so I need to write something here that will satisfy her. Mum, you're amazing. You raised me with patience and love even though I have been, without doubt, your most troublesome child. You're my best friend and my absolute idol. I only hope I can become half the woman and mother you are. That should do it.

In all seriousness though, my parents made me the person I am; they encouraged me to dream, to create, to act, to pretend, to believe in everything.

As ever, I also need to thank my darling, patient husband, and our two gorgeous boys. You three are my biggest fans, my inspiration, my motivation, and the most wonderful of distractions. You help me keep at least one foot on the ground.

And thank you to Sylvia for the hours of free childcare and soft play sessions that gave me the time I needed to complete this book.

Thanks also to Ben, my cover designer, my brother, and something of a kindred spirit. You can turn the thoughts in my head into solid, real life models in a way no one else ever could.

And thank you to everyone else who has helped along the way, probably in ways you didn't even notice. Your belief, your support, your interest, it means everything to me.

www.ingramcontent.com/pod-product-compliance
Lightning Source LLC
Chambersburg PA
CBHW032142170626
46808CB00006B/2333